TEMPTED BY SIN

A DARK STALKER ROMANCE

BOOK ONE

BELLA MOONDRAGON

For Ericilia

CONTENTS

CHAPTER ONE

Paetyn

"How is she doing on the new medication? There haven't been any complications, have there?"

Dr. Charles Barney shakes his head. Strands of thin silver hair fall over his pale brown eyes. He makes no move to push them out of his line of sight, instead choosing to ignore their existence and look down at the chart gripped firmly in his hands. "As of right now, she's responding well to the chemotherapy, but we will ensure we keep a close eye on her at all times. If anything goes wrong with the process and we need to go down a different path of treatment, you'll be the first to know, Paetyn. The cancer is different this time. Stronger. But… we'll figure it out."

I breathe a sigh of relief, my shoulders slumping ever so slightly. Knowing that Mom is being taken care of by the wonderful team at the hospital, led by Dr. Barney, brings a sense of peace I have been searching for since the moment she was admitted many months ago. Taking care of a parent is hard enough for anyone because they don't want to see their loved one in a situation that requires such care from

"

their child. But it's a whole different ballpark taking care of a cancer-filled parent who loves you too much to want you to see them like that—sick and afraid.

Mom knew something was wrong with her for quite some time before she decided to go in and get tested to see what was going on the first time she started feeling bad, about five years ago. She was a busy woman with a corporate job in marketing, going on dates after my father left her a few years before that, with a jam-packed social life. A woman like that doesn't want to admit that something is wrong with her. To admit that is to realize that the life you once knew, filled with fun and exciting times, was probably never going to be the same again. She beat cancer once before, but now it is back with a vengeance.

"Thank you," I say softly, forcing a smile. It's hard to smile when my mom is going through chemotherapy for ovarian cancer. "Knowing you're taking care of her puts my mind at ease, so thank you."

Dr. Barney pats my shoulder, his smile tight. "It's no problem, really. Your mother is in good hands with us." He stands upright, his eyes focused on mine. In an apologetic tone, he says, "These treatments are very expensive but well worth it."

I swallow hard, trying not to reveal the worry that zapped through my body seeing the amount of digits at the end of the bill I'd recently received. We've managed to pay all the previous bills, with the help of my fiancé, but it is still scary every time I get a massive bill like that. "Yes, they are expensive. Rest assured that the bill will be paid on time."

Dr. Barney nods uncomfortably. I'm sure he wasn't trying to imply I wouldn't pay the bill, but I've always been touchy about such things, especially since Mom's insurance had lapsed right before she was diagnosed.

Before the doctor can respond, a nurse taps him on the shoulder, calling him away to another patient. He bids me goodbye before rushing away in the opposite direction. I watch the back of his head until he's no longer in view. He's a rather young-looking man, possibly in his late to mid-forties. But the gray hairs indicate how much he has aged from this job, which is fair enough. Working in the healthcare sector is no easy task.

I hesitate before entering my mom's room. Closing my eyes, I slow my breathing, not wanting her to see the stress and worry I'm sure is written all over my face. Mom is a strong person, so I need to be the same.

The door to the private room creaks open. Mom is propped up in bed watching television, her pale blue eyes focused on the tiny screen protruding from the wall opposite her. She mindlessly braids the ends of her blonde hair before untying the knots and starting again. It's a habit I've seen her do many times when I was a child. After three rounds of chemo, her hair is starting to thin considerably and is falling out in places, but it doesn't stop her from playing with what hair she does have left. When she loses all of her hair completely, she will have to find something else to fidget with.

As I walk further into the room, her eyes snap to meet mine. They light up instantly, and a smile curves her plump lips. "My sweet, Pae. I thought I wasn't going to see you today."

I pull out the chair beside her bed and settle down, ignoring how cold the plastic feels against my clothed thighs. One of the things I despise most about hospitals is how goddamn cold it is here. Would it kill them to turn the heat up a little? Especially during winter.

"I managed to get off work early and thought I would stop by to see you." My eyes scan over the white hospital gown hanging off her frail torso and the crease lines forming at the corners of her eyes and lips. She appears much older and more frail than a normal fifty-year-old woman. Having cancer will often do that to a person. "How are you feeling after this round of treatment?"

Mom waves me off with her hand. "I'm fine, sweetie. You don't need to worry about me. The team here are taking great care of me." She shifts in her spot and reaches out for my hand, which I gladly extend. She feels warm in my grasp, reminding me of when I was a little girl and would only find comfort in the touch of my mother's hand. I still feel that way even as a twenty-six-year-old woman. "Tell me what's new with you. How's work and that fiancé of yours?"

"Work is fine. I have gained a lot of new clients over the past few weeks due to our other office branch closing, so that has been keeping me busy."

She smiles. "You're such a hard worker, Pae. Always have been. I remember when you were just ten years old, you told me how much you wanted to help people. I thought at the time you meant as a medical doctor or something. Turns out you are an up-and-coming psychologist in New York City. You're so close to making it big, sweetheart. I couldn't be prouder."

"It's nothing, really." I love to hear my mother's praises as she has always been my number one supporter all through high school, university, and the many placements I had to do to get to where I am now. But at the same time, I don't enjoy talking about myself in that way. I'm proud of myself, don't get me wrong, but I'm more of a quiet achiever.

"How is Liam?" She changes the subject upon seeing my reluctance to talk about myself and my career. "I haven't seen him for a little while. Is everything okay?"

Ah, yes. Liam. My fiancé.

"He's good. Just busy with the campaign. I'm sure you've seen him a lot on the news lately." The smile on my face doesn't quite reach my eyes speaking about my fiancé. "He did ask me to tell you hello. With his campaign in full swing at the moment, he finds it hard to get away from the campaign trail on time most days. But we're doing good."

"How is the wedding planning?" she asks, giddiness in her voice. "I know I haven't been able to help as much as I would like to, but just know that I'm always here to offer any advice you may need." She licks her lips and squeezes my hand gently. "Believe it or not, your father and I had a wonderful wedding. We may have gotten married young, but we still had the best night."

The mention of my father sends a jolt of hurt straight to my heart, cracking at the edges just a little more. Him leaving my mother three years ago for a woman he worked with hurt more than I thought it would. Not only did he have an affair, but he chose to cut us both out of his life because his new girlfriend told him to. The fact that he was willing to do it, to never speak to his wife or daughter again one random Tuesday afternoon, was heartbreaking. I couldn't believe it.

My mom put on a brave face for both of us, but I could see how deep his betrayal went. She was good at hiding her feelings from everyone around her, but I could read her like a book. She was hurt and angry. But she hid it from everyone, not wanting to appear weak or broken. But I knew how she really felt. He hurt us both, but at least we had each other to lean on.

"Well, we're still trying to figure out what flavor cake we want and how to arrange the flowers," I say. "Any suggestions on what we should do?"

A smile lights up her face as she begins talking about different cake options and flower arrangements we could go with based on what she did for her wedding and the many articles she has read while lying in this hospital bed. Although I'm terrified for her and what her future will look like, the comfort and peace I feel at this moment, talking and laughing together like nothing is wrong, is enough to distract me from reality lurking in the corner of the room.

* * *

The cold wind slaps against my cheeks and nose the moment I step through the front doors of the hospital. Winter in New York City means freezing temperatures at night that require many layers of clothing to bring even a sliver of warmth to your cold body. It's one of the many reasons why I tend to rush home after work. I would much rather be cuddled up on the sofa in front of the fireplace than shivering in the light dusting of snow falling from the sky.

But seeing my mom was important. I would do anything for her, even brave the freezing temperatures.

The parking lot is almost empty as I trudge toward my car, my arms wrapped tightly around my chest to create some warmth. When I arrived after work, the lot was jam-packed with cars, forcing me to park at the very back in one of the last free spaces. While it is annoying having to walk so far to the front doors, I am grateful for the moments of silence it gave me before having to face Dr. Barney. But now I'm just cold, tired, and ready to get home.

When my car comes into my line of sight, a cold shiver races down my spine, stopping me in my tracks. The shiver isn't caused by the wind and snowflakes lashing across my skin. No, that kind of shiver is caused by unwanted eyes watching from the shadows. Stalking, even. The kind of stare that makes a person's entire body freeze with fear.

My heart hammers harshly against my rib cage as my eyes slowly scan the parking lot. The area is mostly dark besides the few street lamps illuminating the large space. There are plenty of dark areas for someone to hide in, waiting for me to get close enough so they can snatch me up and steal me away without anyone noticing.

The thought sends another chill racing down my spine.

Without so much as thinking through my next movements, I take off running toward my car, not caring if the person watching me follows too. All I need to do is get to the safety of my car and lock the doors, shutting them out completely. It's not much of a plan, nor is it a smart one, but it's the only option I have. There is not a chance I'm going to risk staying out here with whoever is lurking around.

Blood rushes in my ears as I race toward my little black 2009 Nissan. The headlights flash at me as I use the key fob to unlock the car. My fingers shake as I yank the door handle harshly and slide into the comfort of the front seat. Within seconds, the locks slip into place, and silence settles over me.

Adrenaline coursing through my veins has my heart beating erratically. Scanning the parking lot, I don't see any signs of movement. I frown, wondering if I had made up the feeling of someone watching me. But that doesn't make sense because the shiver I felt down my spine has never failed me in dangerous or uncertain situations.

Just when I think I'm going crazy, ready to convince myself I dreamt up the entire scenario, my eye catches someone standing under the dim streetlamp across the parking lot. I squint in an attempt to get a better look at whoever it is I'm seeing. The outline appears to be that of a man, but he's unmoving, his body as rigid as a statue. From where I'm sitting in my car, his face is covered by something, concealing his features. A mask, maybe?

"What the hell?" I murmur, unable to believe what I'm seeing. My heart races so fast I fear it might burst through my chest and land on my lap.

It's when the man tilts his head to the side, his body facing my direction, that I realize this man *is* watching *me* and not just an innocent person waiting for someone to come out of the hospital.

Oh, *shit*.

My fingers fumble the car keys in my hand, shaking so badly that my whole body begins to vibrate. With some effort, I slide the key in and twist, roaring the cold engine to life. I don't bother waiting for the car to warm up before my foot presses down on the gas pedal, lurching my car forward.

I try not to look at the person watching me from across the lot, but curiosity gets the better of me. As I'm about to turn out of the exit lane and onto the main road, I catch sight of the mask covering his face, my blood running cold. The base of the mask is black with dark red crosses over the eyes and what appears to be stitching over the mouth, set into a wide, menacing grin.

Even as I speed out of the parking lot, my tires screeching as I go, I still feel his eyes piercing through my skin, my soul. Exhaling a shaky breath, I glance in the rearview mirror to see he's *still* watching me.

CHAPTER TWO

Paetyn

My heart rate hasn't slowed down since the incident in the parking lot. Even as I drive further away, leaving the man standing under the streetlamp in my rearview, my heart continues to pound painfully against my rib cage, pulsating in my ears.

Who was that man? And why did it feel as though his eyes were piercing through my soul from behind that mask?

The car rolls to a stop in the driveway, and for the first time in twenty minutes, I exhale sharply. My lungs burn from holding onto a breath I hadn't managed to release, and I gasp for fresh air to fill my lungs. I close my eyes and drop my hands from the steering wheel. Images of the masked man flash in my mind, sending a cold shiver racing across my skin and down my spine.

Forget about it, Pae, I tell myself. Dwelling on the details of the incident isn't going to change the fact that it happened. All I can do is be thankful that the man didn't get close to me and that I'm home safe.

Now that my breathing has calmed down slightly, I grab my handbag and get out of the car. The night air is crisp against the exposed skin of my cheeks. However, I'm grateful for the chill because they were on fire the moment I got in the car and sped away.

As I approach the front door, the flickering lights from within the window indicate Liam is home. It's odd because I'm usually home before him considering he spends a lot of late nights in the office as of late.

When I enter the house, I make sure to lock the door behind me as quickly as I can. The thought of that man somehow tracking me down and coming up from behind me only to snatch me away before I can alert Liam is not something I want to risk.

"Liam, I'm home," I call out, my voice echoing across the foyer.

"In here," he responds from the living room to my right. "I'm just watching TV."

I kick off my shoes beside Liam's haphazardly discarded leather loafers and walk over to the doorway to the living room. The house Liam bought before we got together has too many rooms for me to count, let alone clean in one day. When he invited me over after our first date, I was shocked to learn the house had three living areas, six bedrooms, and eight bathrooms. The kitchen was larger than the apartment I was living in at the time, and it even had a media room with recliners, a bar, and a popcorn and candy station. It was as if I had just walked into a movie theater and not a room in a normal house.

The home is beautiful, to say the least. It's far beyond anything I ever saw myself living in, especially in a city like New York. But it's far too big for two people. A house of this size would make sense for a large family, but Liam and I are nowhere near having kids right now. He does, however, enjoy showing off such an extravagant house to his friends and campaign sponsors whenever they're invited over for dinner. Liam loves being the center of attention, and I must admit, he does shine under the spotlight. He was born for it.

Liam is sitting on the leather couch with his arm lying across the back of it and his ankle resting on his knee. When he notices my presence by the doorway, his gray eyes pull away from whatever is playing on the television to meet mine. He smiles, although it doesn't quite reach his eyes. It wouldn't be the first time.

"You're home early," I comment as I walk across the room toward him. When I reach him, I bend down to plant a kiss on his chaste lips. The stale scent of women's perfume clings to the collar of his shirt. It's faint but noticeable. It's a scent I have grown used to smelling whenever my fiancé returns home most evenings.

I've had my suspicions about what Liam might be up to while he's supposed to be at work. No matter how many times I ask him about the perfume, he reassures me that it's nothing. His explanation is the scent likely transfers to his clothing from the women he works with at the office. While it could have some truth to it, I'm skeptical.

I don't want to believe my fiancé—who proposed to me six months ago—is cheating on me, but I'm also not blind to the evidence staring me directly in the face. A couple of weeks ago, a woman whose name I didn't know found me on social media. She messaged me with details of a night she spent with Liam. It was a weekend he had been "out of town" for work. While the message came as a shock, I already knew deep in my heart that Liam was hiding something from me.

But despite all the evidence stacked against him, I can't find it in myself to confront him about what I was told. Why? Well, part of me is afraid of his reaction. Liam has a bit of a temper, which I've seen many times since we've been dating. It's not something I want to be on the receiving end of, and I know that if I were to accuse him of cheating on me, he wouldn't be able to hold back his temper.

But that's not the only reason. Keeping my mouth shut is my only option, especially if I want to keep the continued financial support he offers for my mother's medical bills. My paychecks as a fairly new psychologist aren't terrible, but it's certainly not enough to support such extensive bills since my mother has no insurance. Liam comes from a wealthy family who has more money than they know what to do with. His father is an established politician, and his mother is the CEO of Aster Pharmaceutical. Not only do they provide their son with an abundance of money and a recognizable name to help him win elections, but they would do anything for him. And I mean *anything*.

If I want to continue living a comfortable life, it's in my best interest to keep my mouth shut and pick my battles. I need to think about my mother to ensure she gets the best possible care for her condition. Without Liam in my life, it would be rather hard to give her that comfort.

"I managed to get away early," he says, watching me as I take a step back. The skin between his brows creases as his eyes roam over my face. It's almost as if he's searching for something. Can he see the fear from earlier lingering on my features? "Is everything okay, Pae?"

Not wanting him to learn that I'm still shaken up over what happened earlier and the scent of the perfume on his collar makes me nauseous, I force a smile. "I'm fine. Just tired from work is all."

Liam nods slowly and runs a hand through his dirty blond hair. "You work hard, Pae. Pour yourself a glass of wine and relax a little, okay?"

"Yeah, okay." I throw my thumb over my shoulder in the direction of the kitchen. "I'm going to cook pasta for dinner. Do you want a glass of wine while you wait?"

He grins and leans forward to wrap his hand around the back of my thigh. His fingers skim the curve of my ass before he grabs a handful of the skin and squeezes hard. "You know me so well, darling."

* * *

Cutlery clinking against porcelain plates echoes across the large kitchen. Liam is devouring the creamy chicken pasta on his plate, but I'm unable to stomach the food. The incident with the man earlier tonight plays through my mind, making my stomach twist painfully.

The more I think about him, the more I realize I could have been in serious danger had I not gotten to my car as quickly as I did. If he had gotten his hands on me… well, I wouldn't be sitting here with my fiancé eating this delicious meal.

I keep coming back to the same question: *Why?* Why me?

"Pae, what's on your mind?" My eyes snap up at the same time Liam lowers his fork and wipes his mouth with the napkin from his lap. "You've barely touched your food, and you seem lost in thought."

I swallow hard. "I'm okay, I promise."

He gives me a pointed look. "I've known you for four years, Pae. I can tell when something is wrong. So, spill it. What's on your mind?"

"Okay." I lower my silverware and exhale slowly. "Well, when I was walking to my car after work I felt like someone was watching me. It was… unnerving, to say the least. I made a beeline for my car and once I was safely inside, I noticed a man standing next to a streetlamp nearby. I couldn't get a good look at him because he was wearing a mask. It scared the crap out of me though."

His eyes widen ever so slightly before they lower. "A man, you say? Did he approach you at all?"

I shake my head. "We didn't interact, but I could tell he was watching me. Waiting for me even. I was totally freaked out."

He reaches across the dining table to take my hand in his. His skin is cold, despite the warmth from the heater, but I ignore the frigidity and squeeze his hand. "You have nothing to be worried about, Pae. Whoever he is… I will protect you from him, okay? When you're with me, you're safe. Besides, maybe it was just some kid trying to scare you to impress his friends."

I want to tell him that the build of the man watching me was not that of a teenager, but I keep the thought to myself. While I appreciate Liam's sentiment in wanting to ensure he is able to protect me if someone were to ever try and hurt me, I know that deep down if push came to shove, Liam wouldn't be able to hold his own against a perpetrator.

Liam may not have a strong build or lots of muscles, and at times can be a little wimpy, but it doesn't make me love him any less. I know deep down he believes he could protect me, but I know that isn't the case.

I smile at him. "Thank you, darling."

At that moment, Liam's phone started vibrating on the table beside him. He snatches his hand away from mine to check the caller ID. His eyes find mine as he points to the device in his hand. "Sorry, Pae, but I have to take this."

"Take your time."

I watch him stand from the table and walk out of the room. His voice travels down the hallway as he takes the call, leaving me alone in the dining room.

Slumping back in the chair, I sigh heavily. My stomach growls, but my appetite is completely gone. I hate wasting food, but right now, the thought of eating what's on my plate is nauseating.

As I'm pushing around the food on the plate, I hear Liam's voice rise with anger. That captures my attention. I still my hands and listen intently, hoping to catch part of the conversation. I'm not one to eavesdrop on him, especially if it's a work-related call, but I'm also curious. He doesn't share too many details about his campaign for a seat in the Senate other than how he's doing in the polls, the candidates he's up against, and other minor details about working with his father.

After the media caught wind of some images circulating of Liam at college parties in some rather unflattering positions—mostly him passed out on the front lawn of a fraternity—his position in the polls dropped, despite having his father's last name. Not even his father could dig him out of that faux pas.

Liam's voice is slightly muffled, but somehow, I swear I hear him say, "All I need is a few days, and I'll be everyone's hero."

What he's referring to, I have no idea.

His footsteps echoing down the hallway have my back straightening and my eyes turning downward to focus on the plate of uneaten food in front of me.

He exhales heavily when he enters the room and slides back onto the chair across from me. When I look up, he runs a hand through his hair, frustration consuming his features.

I clear my throat. "Is everything okay?"

He doesn't meet my eyes as he nods. "I'm down in the polls and need to boost my campaign to drive in voters. But it's nothing for you to worry about, Pae."

* * *

STARING AT THE DARK CEILING HAS GROWN BORING. THE LONGER I stare, unable to fall into the realm of sleep, the more restless I become. Liam fell asleep hours ago after we had sex, but I haven't been able to follow suit, instead lying awake, eyes wide and mind racing.

With a sigh, I fling the duvet back and slide out of bed. The hardwood floorboards are cold against my feet as I walk to the closed bedroom door. Liam is snoring softly as I open the door and pad quietly down the hallway. I'm not sure a glass of water will help me sleep, but I need to do something to distract the racing thoughts circling my mind.

The kitchen is pitch black save for the moonlight shining in through the window above the sink. I grab a glass from the cabinet above the stove before walking over to the sink. The silence in the room is almost eerie and does nothing to soothe the anxiety coursing through me at this moment.

"Get a grip, Pae," I mumble to myself as water fills the glass. "You're okay. You're safe."

When the glass is full, I turn the tap off and lift it to my lips, ready to chug the entire thing. But something catches my eye through the window, halting my movements. My heart begins to race as I scan the backyard. The same shiver I felt in the parking lot races down my spine again. The glass in my hand trembles, but I make no move to put it down.

He's *here*.

Moments later, I find him. He's standing under the large tree in the backyard with his hands shoved deep into the back of the black pants hanging from his hips. The moonlight shining across the yard allows me a better view of him. I'm unable to see his face as it's still covered by a mask and is hidden in the shadows, but I notice his torso and the hard muscles protruding from the black T-shirt clinging to his chest. His right arm is littered with tattoos, but I'm unable to make out the designs, and inky strands of dark hair frame his face, wavy in texture, adding to the intensity of his presence.

Blood rushes in my ears, and my heart pounds harshly against my rib cage. The glass of water slips from my hands, smashing to pieces at the bottom of the sink. The impact sends a shattering noise throughout the kitchen, likely traveling far enough to reach Liam in the bedroom. But I don't move. I *can't* move. His eyes are holding me hostage, pinning me to where I stand. I may not be able to see them, but I can *feel* them.

I grip the edge of the sink for support, my knees wobbling beneath me. The urge to run to Liam and have him protect me screams at me, but my feet are unable to move. My spine is rigid as I stare ahead, unable to tear my eyes away from him. I convince myself to commit as many details about him to memory as possible so that I can relay them to Liam if something were to happen.

For some odd reason, I find myself unable to look away from him because I'm curious. Why is he here? What does he want with me? It's clear he has an agenda in mind. Otherwise, he wouldn't have waited for me after work or tracked me down at my home.

If he wants to hurt me, then what is he waiting for? He could easily enter through the back door and execute whatever plan he has in mind, but instead, he's waiting for me intently. But why? What is he doing?

Rushing footsteps down the staircase tear my eyes away from the man.

"Pae? Are you okay?" Liam calls out, his voice thick with sleep.

"I'm fine," I murmur, my mind whirling.

When I turn back to look at the man, he's gone. And for some odd reason, my heart sinks a little.

Who is he, and what does he want with me?

CHAPTER THREE

Paetyn

THE VOICE OF THE CLIENT SITTING ACROSS FROM ME IS SLIGHTLY muffled by the rampant thoughts of the masked man racing through my mind. It has been two days since I saw him standing in my backyard, his eyes piercing me through the mask covering his features, and I haven't stopped thinking about him.

Liam told me not to worry about him, but how can I possibly not? It's one thing to watch me from across the parking lot, but it's another to stand in the darkness of my backyard and watch me like a hawk, making his presence known. He's keeping his features concealed for a reason, so I'm unable to identify him, but if he's going out of his way to let me know he's there, watching me, then why hasn't he made a move yet? What is he waiting for?

The thought of him doing something to hurt me sends a shiver across my body, goosebumps pebbling my skin from beneath the cardigan wrapped tightly around my torso. I haven't been able to sleep much the past two days for fear that I would see him in my dreams. He hasn't shown himself since the night in the parking lot, but that doesn't mean he isn't around, watching me from the shadows. When walking to my car now, I call my mom as a distraction from the anxiety squeezing my heart. She has been more than happy to talk with me, so that has eased the tension in my shoulders a little.

But it doesn't erase the fear that the masked man is going to appear out of nowhere at any time.

"Miss Jones, are you okay?"

My eyes snap up to the client across from me. Jayden is a young man in his early twenties battling depression and anxiety. He was one of my first clients after I became a registered psychologist and has been coming to see me once a week to talk through his feelings and thoughts. He has a lot on his plate with his home life, so the fact that I haven't been listening to him, lost in my own thoughts, makes my stomach twist painfully.

I adjust my position in the chair and clear my throat. Guilt claws its way up my throat as I force a smile onto my lips. "I'm okay, yes. Apologies, Jayden. Can you please repeat yourself?"

Jayden nods and repeats his words, detailing an incident that happened with his father recently. Jayden's father isn't a good man, to put it simply. He's verbally abusive and doesn't understand his son. My job is to make sure Jayden feels heard and remind him that he's important and his life matters. He matters.

Forget about the masked man, I tell myself. *Your client needs you.*

I get through the rest of the session with Jayden, putting the man in the mask at the back of my mind. Jayden is grateful for my advice as he leaves my office, which eases the guilt swirling in my stomach from the mishap earlier in the session.

With a sigh, I collect my belongings and lock my office for the night. Clarissa is sitting at the receptionist's desk typing away on her obnoxiously loud keyboard. When I step toward her, juggling my phone and car keys in my hand, her brown doe eyes lift from the computer to meet mine.

"Leaving for the night, Pae?" Her voice is soft and gentle, which matches her exterior. Clarissa is freshly nineteen, so her youthful appearance brings a certain calmness to the office. I had my doubts about her to begin with, considering her age and inexperience in the field, but she is great with the clients and is a pleasure to work with.

I stop in front of her desk, meeting her gaze. "I am. Are my clients for tomorrow still available to come in?"

"Your 10:00 A.M. session was canceled an hour ago when you went in with your last client, something about getting food poisoning last night. But the rest of your sessions are good."

Smacking my lips together, I nod. "Thank you, Lissa. You should head home, though. It's getting late."

She waves me off. "I won't be much longer, I promise. Getting ahead on the tasks for the next day is one of the ways I like to stay on top of everything. As soon as I'm done, I will have Jerry escort me out to my car. He's waiting for me out front."

Jerry is her new boyfriend she met a couple of months ago while at a party. They seem to be good together, so I have no doubt he'll keep her safe. I wish I could have my fiancé walk me to my car, but he's a busy man, so that's out of the question.

I smile and nod. "Okay, well, be safe. I'll see you bright and early tomorrow morning."

"Good night, Pae."

On my way out of the building, I spot Jerry leaning against the wall beside the front door and wave at him. He returns the gesture and goes back to playing a golf game on his phone. The sidewalks are busy with people leaving work for the night, so I join the crowd and make the trek to my car.

I'm barely a few steps down the sidewalk when I get a call from my best friend, Raya. Perfect, I have someone to talk to on the phone while I walk, saving me from calling my mother again. The last thing I want to do is bother her when she's recovering from her latest chemo treatment.

"Hey, you," I say into the phone, a smile tipping up the corner of my lips. "Long time, no talk."

"Pae!" Raya calls excitedly into the phone. "How have you been? How is your mom?"

"I'm good, just busy with work as usual. And she's good too. Her most recent round of chemo went smoothly a few days ago, and she's responding well to the new medication she is on, so I'm hopeful she'll be able to beat the cancer."

"God, she's amazing," Raya praises, her voice filled with admiration for my mom. "And I'm glad to hear you're both doing well. I was actually calling to suggest we go out for drinks tomorrow night if you're free. It's a Friday night and I could use a gossip session with my best friend whom I haven't seen in forever."

Raya and I have been friends since middle school. I found her eating lunch in the girls' bathroom because she didn't have anyone to eat with. Much to my surprise, I was also going to eat in the girls' bathroom because my friends at the time decided to ditch me to go sit with the popular boys. So, we decided to sit in the bathroom and eat our lunch together. This turned into eating lunch together every day, sleeping at each other's house every weekend, and getting up to a lot of mischief throughout the rest of our days in school.

Honestly, we still do get up to a lot of mischief, but it's a lot more tamed now that we are both engaged.

"I can make Saturday night work," I respond. "With how busy work has been lately, I could use a drink to unwind a little."

"Now that's what I like to hear," Raya cheers. "No partners, okay?"

Someone bumps into my shoulder roughly, forcing a puff of air from my lips as I gather myself, standing upright. "That shouldn't be a problem. Liam is catching up with his father to meet with some campaign sponsors and whatnot, so I'm all yours."

"Seren is going out for drinks with his work friends, so I'm free as a bird also. He told me to tell you that the four of us need to get together soon for dinner."

The dreaded alleyway comes into view, and my heart begins to race. I swallow hard and focus on Raya's voice and not the blood rushing in my ears. "Yeah, that sounds good to me. Maybe we can host this time since you and Seren went out of your way to prepare such a wonderful dinner for us last time we got together."

"Well, it was more of an engagement dinner considering you had already been engaged for a few months and had decided not to have a party since you were too consumed with planning the wedding. It was the least we could do," she points out. "But speaking of the wedding, how is the planning going?"

I turn the corner, leaving behind the safety net of strangers to keep me company, even if they don't know it. My heart hammers against my rib cage as I walk further into the darkness. I find it hard to focus on Raya's words because of the sense of dread that washes over me. The moment that same shiver I have felt twice now races down my spine, I stop walking, my legs unable to carry me further.

He's here again.

This time, he's standing about thirty feet away from me, his intimidating stance backlit by the street lamps in the parking lot behind him.

"Oh, shit," I breathe, staring at the masked man. My throat is thick with lead, and I'm struggling to get any air into my lungs. "Oh, no."

"Pae?" Raya's voice rings through the phone. "Is everything okay?"

Now that I'm much closer to him, the details of the mask become clearer. The stitching over the eyes and mouth is terrifying, especially when paired with the piercing blue eyes gazing at me from behind the mask. They hold me captive, forcing me to stay where I am. Even if I wanted to run or scream, I couldn't. Not when his stare is so intense.

The masked man tilts his head to the side, his hands clenching and unfurling as he watches me.

"Paetyn?" Raya tries again, panic settling in her tone. "Are you okay? What's going on?"

I lower the phone to my side but don't end the call. My gaze stays on the masked man, my heart about to leap out of my throat. He's wearing the same clothes as two nights ago—a black T-shirt and black jeans. How is this man not freezing? Winter in New York City is no joke.

I swallow hard, my fingers twitching around my phone at my side. If I want to get away from this man alive, I need to do something. *Now*. My best option is to turn and run back to the busy sidewalk. He wouldn't be stupid enough to try and hurt me in the middle of a busy walkway with plenty of eyewitnesses.

Running is my only option at this point. I just pray I'm a faster runner than he is.

Without giving it another thought, I turn on my heels and make a run for the end of the alleyway. I was never the best runner in school, but I'm hoping the adrenaline and fear coursing through my rigid body are enough to propel me forward and away from the danger lurking behind me.

Unfortunately for me, as soon as I start running, the masked man does too. The pounding of his footsteps against the concrete behind me spikes my heart rate to dangerous levels.

He's gaining on me—and quickly.

The blood rushing in my ears intensifies with each step, blocking out Raya's concerned voice calling loudly through the phone gripped tightly in my hand. I just need to make it to the end of the alley, and I'll be okay. If I make it out of this alleyway, he won't be able to—

I scream the moment a pair of strong arms wrap tightly around my waist. I'm feet away from the safety of the busy sidewalk, but that joy is ripped away from me as I'm pulled back into the depths of hell. Any hope I had of surviving this man has vanished into thin air.

My phone clatters to the ground. Raya hasn't stopped calling my name the entire time.

"Let go of me!" I cry, clawing at the skin on his forearms in the hopes it'll get me out of his hold. But it doesn't work. "Help! Someone help me!"

The man doesn't say a word as he hauls me down the alleyway, my back pressed firmly against his chest. He doesn't seem fazed by the struggle I'm putting up. But I don't stop. If I stop fighting, I'm dead.

A wave of sandalwood and nicotine assaults my senses before something wet covers my mouth and nose. My body goes limp in his arms as all the fight leaves me, followed by what I'm sure is the depths of hell—darkness as far as the eye can see.

CHAPTER FOUR

Paetyn

For a split second, my brain convinces me I'm blind. Darkness surrounds me, engulfing me whole and holding me hostage. But the soft buzzing working its way into the depths of my mind tells me that I haven't been completely dragged down to the depths of hell with no sight of return.

Not yet, at least.

My head thumps painfully, the source coming from deep behind my eyes. The rhythmic movement echoes in my ears, making it hard to think straight. I try my best to force my hand up to cradle my head, hoping it'll ease the pain, but my limbs are heavy. Too heavy to move.

With a groan, I fight against the pain coursing through my body to force my eyes open. At first, it's almost painful. My eyelids feel as though they've been glued shut, keeping me from seeing. But with a great deal of effort, I pry them open and am immediately assaulted by a warm, orange glow above me.

A hiss slips past my lips as I fight to clear my vision. The sudden intrusion of light hitting my eyes only intensifies the pounding in my skull. Everything hurts.

But why?

Why does my body feel as though it's on fire and weighs as much as a cement truck?

My limbs seem to be working now because I'm able to bring my elbow under me to prop my body up. I blink rapidly to clear my vision and focus on calming my heavy breathing. When my surroundings become clear, my heart rate spikes all over again.

Where the hell am I?

With my heart in my throat, I gaze down at the thin white sheets wrapped haphazardly around my jean-clad legs. The mattress beneath me is dirty and has seen better days. What shocks me the most is the thick chain cuffed around my ankle, keeping me a hostage of the twin bed. The metal is rusted and looks as though it has been around for many years.

The sleeves of my long-sleeved blouse are rolled up to my elbows, exposing me to the chill in the air. Out of the corner of my eye, I find the coat I was wearing when I left work folded neatly on the floor.

My eyes snap up to gaze around the rest of the room lit only by a single bulb hanging overhead. I fear if I make any sudden movements, whoever brought me here will come barging into the room. The boarded-up window above the small bed I lie on is almost mocking me—a reminder that it's my only way of escaping this small room.

Heavy breathing sounds from across the room, and at that moment, my heart almost slams through my rib cage. Without so much as moving a muscle, I drag my eyes away from the window to the single chair situated in the corner opposite the bed, beside the only door to the room.

The masked man I have been seeing the past few days sits in the black leather chair silently, his long legs spread out in front of him. He's so silent as he regards me, his hands clasped together in his lap. I feel his gaze upon me from behind the barrier he uses to keep his identity hidden.

A cold chill races down my spine. Just like every other time I have encountered him.

I open my mouth to speak, but the words get caught in my dry throat, unable to make their escape. My throat works to relieve the dryness as I swallow hard. I'm unable to take my eyes off the masked man for fear that if I let him out of my sight, he might attack.

"Wh-who are you?" My voice is small, barely above a whisper. But he heard me. The slight tilt of his head gives him away. "Why d-did you take me?"

The memory of him cornering me in the alleyway on my way home from work blasts through my mind like a home movie, replaying the moment he caught me, his strong arms wrapped tightly around my waist as he dragged me into the depths of darkness I couldn't escape.

I had no real chance of getting away from him. But I had hoped someone would save me. Anyone. And now I'm here, chained to a bed, while he watches me intently, not saying a goddamn word.

"Please let me go home." My hands shake more and more with each word. I manage to push myself into a seated position, ignoring the way my bones creak with the simple movement. "I have a fiancé who will be looking for me."

The masked man snorts, the sound deep, but doesn't say anything. He just stares at me, inky curls spilling around from behind the mask. Waiting. Watching. The silence is almost suffocating, squeezing my lungs so tightly I'm unable to force air into my lungs.

What does he want from me?

Who the hell is this man?

Dampness stings the hairs in my nostrils, and I have to force back a gag at the terrible scent. The room smells wet like it's been flooded previously and the odor hasn't been removed. It's a vast contrast to the floral candles I burn every night at home because Liam says he likes the light fragrance.

Liam.

Oh, God. I'm sure he's worried sick about me. At least, I hope he is. When I was taken from the alleyway, Raya was still on the phone, so I'm sure she has informed Liam about what happened. He would have gone to the police right away when I didn't come home. I'm sure of it.

Knowing that people are out there searching for me gives me a small moment of comfort. But it's ruined by the masked man staring silently at me. The muscles in his biceps flex slightly as if he's clenching his fists momentarily. Despite the slight chill in the air, he's still wearing a black T-shirt with his black jeans. It's as if the cold doesn't affect him at all.

"Are you doing this for ransom?" I ask, my voice raspy. My heart pounds in my chest with each second ticking by without hearing a single word from my kidnapper. "Are you going to kill me? Sell me into sex trafficking? What do you want from me?"

Panic seeps into my pores at the thought of either of those scenarios happening. This could go either way; I could live, or I could die, and the thought of the latter terrifies me.

What if I don't make it home alive?

The masked man keeps his mouth shut. He stands from the chair and cracks his knuckles, his eyes searing into my skin from behind the mask. At the sight of the scars on his knuckles—an indicator that he uses his fists quite a bit—I cower against the metal frame headboard, hoping it'll put some distance between us.

But instead of moving in my direction, he turns to the door, unlocks the latch, and steps through it. When the door closes behind him, I hear what sounds like a lock clicking into place, trapping me inside.

Even though my head is spinning and my limbs are heavy, I know this might be one of my only chances to find an escape route. He could come back with a decision about my fate—one that doesn't allow me to see the light of morning. I take this moment of silence as an opportunity to spring from the bed.

The wooden floorboards squeak beneath the weight of my feet. I cringe at the sound, hoping the masked man didn't hear it from wherever he has gone. I could be locked in a little cabin in the middle of the woods or a basement in a house on a suburban street.

The possibilities are endless. Either way, I need to get the hell out of here.

I try to explore the space around the twin bed, but the chain around my ankle only lets me get so far before I'm helpless to move anywhere else. But the small give in the chain does allow me to inspect the window above the bed. It's boarded up with old planks of wood, not allowing so much as a sliver of light to peek through it. Which means I'm unable to inspect the surroundings outside.

"Goddamn it," I groan, frustration prickling my skin. "This is useless."

The lock on the door sliding open sends my heart plummeting to the bottom of my feet. I whirl around just in time to see the masked man entering the room with a tray of food. The scent of cold deli ham wafts through the air, mixing with the damp smell. The odor of food instantly makes my stomach growl with hunger, reminding me I have no idea what day it is or how long I've gone without eating.

He sets the tray on the end of the mattress with easy strides before turning to stand in front of the closed door. I feel his eyes on me as he clasps his hands together in front of him, his body straight and rigid.

I look between him and the ham sandwich and bottle of water on the tray. "Is that for me?"

He doesn't so much as give me a nod, but the tilt of his head is answer enough.

I eye the bottle of water, desperate to quench the thirst clawing at my throat. The thought that he could have slipped some sort of drug into the water crosses my mind. But as much as I would like to deny his offer of food purely so I can keep my senses about me, the violent growl of my stomach gives me away.

I'm starving and thirsty. And if I want to keep my energy up to have a fighting chance of escaping this room, I need to get something in me.

My body vibrates with nerves as I lower onto the edge of the mattress. The sandwich shakes slightly in my trembling hands as I bring it to my mouth. I don't bother inspecting the food before I take a bite. The moment the ham and cheese touch my taste buds, I'm unable to stop myself from taking large bites, desperate to fill the ache in my stomach. He's added lettuce, mayo, and tomato, too, as if he knows how I like my ham sandwiches. Lucky guess.

With each bite I take, I feel my kidnapper's intense gaze searing a hole into my skin. It sends a shiver down my spine.

I wish I knew what he was thinking or why he brought me here in the first place. Not knowing what's going to happen to me is a terrifying feeling. He could do whatever he wanted to me in the blink of an eye, and I wouldn't be able to do anything about it. But instead, he's watching me eat the food he offered, not saying a single word.

It's unnerving, really.

Within two minutes, the sandwich is gone and the bottle of water is mostly empty. Eating so fast has given me a stomachache, but it's better than the feeling of being hungry. Even though I'm still thirsty, I know I need to preserve the water for as long as possible since I don't know if he's going to give me more or not.

He steps forward to collect the tray with his tattooed arm. Instinct has me scrambling back on the bed, my eyes fixed on every tiny movement he makes.

He stands to his full height, towering over me with the red tray gripped firmly in his hands. Just when I think he's going to turn around and leave, an unexpected deep voice sounds from behind the Halloween-esque mask that sends a shiver down my spine.

"Don't even think about trying to escape. You won't get far."

CHAPTER FIVE

Paetyn

How does a person determine how much time has passed without seeing a sliver of sunlight?

No matter how hard I try to keep track of time by counting each second as I feel them ticking by, committing the numbers to memory as best I can, I'm still clueless as to how long I've been sitting on this thin mattress with a dirty sheet wrapped around me, praying that Liam will come to my rescue.

Is my fiancé worried about me? Is he doing everything in his power to find me?

God, I hope so.

The longer I sit here, wondering what the masked man is going to do to me, the more I begin to lose hope of being rescued. I could be anywhere in the country right now, making it near impossible for Liam to find me. If the house I'm being held in is located deep in the woods, I may as well begin digging my own grave.

I feel so helpless. So confused. And so fucking angry that I'm unable to see my mother.

Picturing her face when I close my eyes brings the sense of comfort I'm desperately seeking, but it's also a reminder that she is likely confused about why I haven't visited or called on my way home from work like I do most days. The thought of her thinking I have abandoned her....

I swallow the lump in my throat, my lips quivering. Crying isn't an option. I refuse to appear weak in front of my kidnapper. I'm sure it's what he wants—to see my fear. He probably gets off on it.

What I don't understand about the man who kidnapped me is why he's treating me like a house guest, minus the filthy bed and the chain secured around my ankle preventing me from leaving. He routinely brings me food and water but makes no effort to speak to me. Not even when he releases my ankle from the chain attached to the bed and escorts me to the bathroom attached to the room. The words he uttered about not being able to leave ring in my head—another reminder of how trapped I am.

Each time I see the mask covering his face, hiding his identity, fear slides across my skin. His presence alone indicates he's a dangerous man. Whenever he enters the room, his shoulders are tense, his body rigid, and his eyes hard as he stares at me from behind the creepy mask. He may scare me, but I'm grateful for the food he offers. I would be in worse condition if he didn't.

He could starve me if he wanted to or do whatever he wants to me. I'm completely helpless. But he doesn't hurt me. He doesn't even speak to me, let alone touch me. Why?

Despite being unable to keep track of time by counting seconds, I have a feeling the masked man is bringing me three meals a day. If that's the case, he has offered me five meals in total, which means I have likely been here for two days.

Two whole fucking days.

I can't believe it.

As if sensing my thoughts about him, the lock on the door unlatches, and the masked man steps through the doorway with the same red tray he has presented me with each time. For my third meal of the day, a steaming Styrofoam cup of ramen sits beside a bottle of water and an apple. It's different from the sandwiches he's been offering.

I watch as he sets the tray on the end of the mattress, the muscles in his arms constricting with the movement. He wears the same thing every day—a black T-shirt, black jeans, and that damn mask. It must be his kidnapper uniform.

The cup of noodles is in my hands before he sits down in the chair across from me, his usual place to watch me eat. He leans back in the chair, stretching his long legs out in front of him.

I ignore his gaze and blow on the steaming water in the cup. With how cold it gets in this room, my hands have long since turned into ice cubes, so the warmth of the cup is greatly appreciated and needed.

Each time he stops by, the masked man sits and watches me eat. Once I'm done, he takes the tray and leaves, not returning until the next meal. Although it's awkward sitting in silence while I eat, I never know what to say to him. What does one say to their kidnapper?

"So…" I begin, still cupping the noodles in my hands, "do you have any family?"

I could punch myself for the stupid question, but I had to say *something*. If I'm going to be spending time with this man, I may as well try to get him talking. The more I learn about him, the more information I can supply the police when they find me.

His body stiffens as his large hands grip the armrests. My question stunned him. But what stuns me more is his response. "No."

It's the first time I have heard him speak since I first woke up here. Now, I just need to keep him talking. Maybe if I can play the sympathy card and remind him that I'm a real person, he might let me walk out of here unscathed.

"I have a family." My voice is soft but determined nonetheless. "I'm an only child. My father left my mother a few years back, and now I'm helping my mom through her second bout of cancer. She needs me."

Silence. But I can feel his eyes piercing through my soul.

I shift slightly on the bed, my heart racing ever so slightly. "I have a fiancé, too. His name is Liam. We met at a club four years ago and have been engaged for two. I do love him, but I don't trust him."

I want to punch myself again for revealing such personal information, but it just slipped out without me realizing it. However, the admission seems to pique the masked man's interest because he sits up straighter, his long fingers twisting the thick silver ring on his left hand. A design is etched into the band, but I can't make it out from here.

The cup of noodles is now forgotten in my hands. The need to get this man talking to me is stronger than my desire to eat. Instead, I allow the cup's warmth to spread across my body.

"I just… I have a sneaking suspicion that he's sleeping around behind my back, but I don't want to say anything because he helps with my mother's medical bills. It's just… complicated."

The man tilts his head to the side, inky curls framing his face. If he wants to say something, he doesn't open his mouth, let alone make a noise. He just… listens.

So, I keep going.

"But despite all that, I still care for him and hope that he's looking for me. He will find me." The words are filled with conviction—a warning to my kidnapper that I will be getting out of this room alive. "If I were you, I would be afraid of getting caught."

And now I've just ruined it. I was supposed to be playing the sympathy card in the hopes I could tug at his heartstrings enough by telling him personal details about me, but now I'm threatening him.

You're an idiot, Pae.

The masked man stands, his body tense with his hands fisted at his side. "I'm not scared of your fiancé, little bird. If anything, he should be afraid of *me*."

And with that, he storms out of the room, slamming the door behind him. My heart races wildly in my chest, the cup of noodles now lukewarm in my hands as I stare after him.

I need to learn when to keep my mouth shut because that interaction did not go the way I planned. Now, I just have to pray that I didn't make my situation worse.

CHAPTER SIX

Paetyn

A DEEP VOICE BOOMS THROUGH THE WOODEN DOOR OF THE ROOM, startling me awake. My heart slams into my throat as I force myself into a seated position, clutching the sheets to my chest.

What the hell is going on?

Even though I've only heard the masked man speak a few times, I recognize his voice. His tone is deep and unlike anything I've ever heard. But who is he talking to? No one responds to him, so I can only assume he's speaking to someone on the phone.

His muffled voice filters throughout the room, but soon his words become clearer as if he's pacing the floor outside, getting closer and closer to the door. The desire burning deep in my chest to know what he's saying consumes me. If I want to know more about this man and potentially learn why I'm here, I need to listen in on the conversation.

Without making a noise, I slide off the creaky mattress, hold the thick chain attached to my ankle in my hand, and walk toward the rotting wooden door. The chain doesn't allow much slack, so I have to settle for standing five feet back. But the distance is enough for me to make out my kidnapper's next words.

"What the hell is taking so long? You told me three days."

Silence.

"I don't give a fuck. You told me three days, man. That's all you get."

Silence.

"We had a deal. I held up my end of the bargain so I suggest you do the same. I'm not afraid to get my hands dirty if you continue to make me wait. I'm not a patient man, so you better hurry the fuck up before I begin to lose what little patience I do possess."

Silence.

"I'm unable to guarantee her safety the longer it takes you to sort your shit out. The clock is ticking, asshole. Either you hurry the fuck up or she's gone."

My brows crease with confusion. Who is he talking to? What is he referring to with the three days comment? And who is he expecting to arrive here?

The questions swirling in my mind make my vision foggy. But it doesn't stop me from continuing to question why I'm here. Why me?

He mumbles some other words before the sound of shuffling shoes makes their way in my direction.

"Shit," I curse, my heart rate spiking.

With the chain gripped firmly in my hands, I race back to the bed and climb atop it, hoping the squeaking springs can't be heard through the door. If I'm caught listening in on his private conversation, it might just be the thing that sends him over the edge. I don't need to give him a reason to hurt me.

Seconds later, the lock unlatches on the door, and it swings open, slamming against the wall behind it. My instinct is to jump, but I would hate to give away my sneakiness because of that. I just need to play it cool and act like I just woke up.

He storms into the room, his intimidating height making me shrink back against the headboard. Oh, god. He knows I was listening, and now he's going to hurt me. I just hope that when he kills me, I'm still recognizable to my mom and Liam. If anything—

My eyes widen when the man walks to the chair in the corner of the room and sits down, spreading his long legs out. His eyes are focused on me, his curls messy around the edge of the mask. For a man who was arguing with someone on the phone moments ago, threatening to potentially hurt me, he's oddly relaxed. But not quite, if his white knuckles gripping the armrests are any indication.

The silence in the room is suffocating. My grip on the sheets tightens as I match his gaze, waiting to see what he wants. This is the first time he's entered the room without a tray of food or gesturing for me to leave to use the bathroom.

"What do you want?" The words are barely audible, sounding as small as they do to my ears. But I had to ask. If he's going to kill me, I would like the chance to prepare myself for what's to come or at least try to fight back. "Are you going to hurt me?"

As usual, he doesn't say anything. He just watches me, his gaze so intense my skin prickles, forming goosebumps in its wake. With the silence building between us, and him making no move to speak or leave, I have no choice but to stare back at him. I refuse to let this man think I'm weak, so if I have to hold his gaze for the next hour, then so be it.

The longer we stare at each other, neither of us moving an inch, the more it fuels the fire simmering deep in my core. I don't know why it ignited or why I haven't put it out yet. Maybe it's the way his thick arms rest on the chair, the tattoos on his right arm on full display, or the taut muscles beneath the thin material of the black T-shirt clinging to his torso. Maybe it's the fact that I've been chained to his bed for who knows how long, and I'm craving a human touch— someone to touch me, kiss me, *please* me.

I'm aware such thoughts about my kidnapper are wrong. Border-line fucked up, even. But I can't get the image of his large hand grazing my hip gently before he pulls my body flush against his, the warmth of his chest radiating through my shirt out of my mind.

I know Liam's face should be the first to come to mind when

having such a fantasy, but it doesn't. No. The face that comes to mind is the one sitting across from me, hidden behind a haunting mask.

What the hell is wrong with me?

My eyes widen when he leans forward on the chair and rests his elbows firmly on his knees, making his biceps bigger than they already were. I swallow hard at the sight, my mouth suddenly dry as if I had stuffed cotton balls inside.

"I know you're thinking about me, little bird."

CHAPTER SEVEN

Paetyn

I BLINK AT HIM, UNABLE TO FORM A SINGLE THOUGHT, LET ALONE A sentence to respond to his comment. The masked man blurs in my vision as I process his insane suggestion.

Thinking about him? Has he lost his damn mind? In what world would I be thinking sexually about the man who kidnapped me, has had me chained to a dingy bed for days, and refuses to speak to me? The thought is insane, that's what it is.

And yet, I feel the dampness between my thighs from my fantasy from moments ago when I thought about him touching me, his large hands caressing my skin, leaving goosebumps in their wake. I shiver at the thought.

Yeah, I'm a fucking liar because I *am* thinking about him, and that's the problem.

But I won't admit that to him, no matter how long he sits there and stares at me with his head tilted to the side as he regards me.

God, I'm pathetic.

"You're wrong," I manage to bite out despite the harsh beating of my heart against my rib cage. "You want to know what I'm thinking about?" He simply clasps his hands together in response. "I'm thinking about how much I'm going to enjoy seeing you behind bars when I'm rescued."

The man snorts, followed by a booming laugh that rattles my insides. It's so deep and sultry that I have to fight from squeezing my thighs together at the sound.

Goddamn.

"Funny, little bird. But I'm sure I could find more enjoyment out of you being chained up. Preferably to my bed while I fuck you until you're screaming my name."

I blanch at his words, my eyes rounding to the size of the moon. The audacity of this man…. Who does he think he is saying something as crude as that? And why does it make my core throb at the thought of it happening?

I swallow hard and shift on the bed, my jaw tense as I stare back at him. "What is your name then, hmm? How could I possibly scream it when I don't know it?"

His jaw ticks as he regards me, his shoulders now tense.

Checkmate, asshole.

If he wants to play this game, then I'm willing to as well. The first day of my captivity, I was a scared kitten filled with anxiety, wondering what would become of me. But the more time I spend with my kidnapper, the tension between us growing, I can't help but consider that maybe he doesn't want to hurt me. If he did, he would've done so by now.

The question of why he kidnapped me still lingers in the back of my mind. But if I'm going to be taken out by this man, whoever he may be, I may as well go down swinging until the very end.

"Who are you?" I ask in a deep voice, grasping onto the boldness blooming in my chest. If I don't, I may never say the things I want to. Now might be my only chance. "Why did you choose me?"

Just like every other time I've questioned him, he doesn't respond. He's as solid as a marble statue as he sits in the chair, elbows resting on his knees, gazing intensely upon me from behind the mask. After a long moment of silence, he runs a hand through his curls and leans back in the chair, silent.

"Why haven't you killed me yet? I mean, you clearly took me for a reason. If it wasn't to kill me or force me into sex trafficking, then what is your plan for me?"

The thought of being smuggled across the country to ultimately meet my fate of working in a brothel for the rest of my days, or being bought and sold by awful, powerful men to do whatever they want to me, makes my skin crawl. I would rather take the option of death than live the rest of my life as a sex prisoner.

"Who do you work for?" I demand, my voice quivering slightly. As much as I want to know if this man is taking orders from a boss who is an even more dangerous man, or if he's simply acting alone, I don't think I can handle the response if he were to speak. "I want to know why I'm here."

He stands, his height intimidating as he looms over the thin mattress. I'm cast in his shadow—not really, but it certainly feels like I am. His jaw ticks as he gazes down at me, unmoving.

The urge to hide under the thin sheets is strong. Any boldness coursing through my veins has disappeared. Despite the fear coating my body, the same fire burning deep within my core lingers, confusing the hell out me.

I need to stop thinking about this. Now. It's wrong.

"You don't want to know who I work for, little bird. But you don't have to worry about me hurting you, unless you ask me to, of course."

My heart leaps into my throat as I watch him turn, my eyes roaming his broad back as he swings the door open and slams it shut behind him. The lock latching into place echoes in my mind— reminding me I'm still trapped in this godforsaken room with no way of escaping.

I close my eyes and attempt to calm my racing heart. No matter how hard I try to forget the sound of his stupid, deep laugh and the way my skin heats beneath his gaze, I can't seem to rid my mind of the damn masked man. Picturing him only fuels the fire burning in my core, aching to be touched.

Thinking about him is wrong, I know this. But I can't stop. Not when he makes me feel like my entire body has just walked through a forest fire. Not even Liam has made me feel that way before.

I swallow hard and lie back on the pillow, the box springs digging into my back. My core aches, and I squeeze my thighs together to relieve the pain. The attempt is futile. All it does is make my head spin and my hand twitch beside me, itching to touch myself.

After a moment of contemplating, I screw my eyes shut, shame washing over me like a tidal wave. My hand has a mind of its own as it slips beneath the sheet and over the front of my T-shirt. The base of my throat thumps with each rapid heartbeat as I slip my hand beneath the waistband of pants.

The moment my fingers brush against my pulsing clit, stars burst in my vision. My head spins as my fingers become coated in my juices. The masked man pops into my mind, consuming me. For a brief moment, as my back arches off the bed and I bite back a moan, I picture his fingers touching me, circling my sensitive pussy with precision like he's done it a million times.

"Shit," I groan lowly, fighting to keep my breath from catching in my throat as I continue to work my clit.

"You like that, don't you, little bird?" I hear his deep voice in the back of my mind, urging me to keep going. Guiding me to release.

A gasp bursts from my throat as I imagine him wrapping his lips around my swollen pussy, licking and sucking like a starved man, desperate for a taste. My back arches off the bed again as the pressure continues to build in my core.

"You like touching yourself to the thought of me, hmm?"

His voice echoes in my head, nearly sending me head first off the cliff. But I manage to hold on to that release as my fingers circle my core, building the pressure with each flick through my folds. I'm all but panting as I chase that release, eager to come at the thought of the masked man being the one to get me off.

"Does being my captive turn you on?"

Every ounce of shame I felt moments ago dissipates, now replaced with lust and desire.

"That's it, little bird. Come for me like the good girl I know you are."

That is all it takes for me to dive off the edge of the cliff with no safety harness on, barreling toward the jagged rocks lying in wait at the bottom. My head spins as I come on my slick fingers. They're a stark reminder of what I just did.

I've barely come down from the high, my vision clearing slightly as I open my eyes and stare at the moldy roof. Guilt consumes me, crashing over me so harshly I struggle to get air into my lungs.

I just got myself off to a man who kidnapped me and chained me to a bed. A man who is not my fiancé.

My hands fly up to rest over my face, and I groan into them. I can't believe I just did that. What the hell is wrong with me? I could blame my actions on being trapped in this room and needing some relief, but thinking about my captor while doing so is next level fucked up. I'm a mess; that's the only explanation I can conjure up. If I analyze the fantasy of being touched by my captor lingering in the back of my mind, I may not like what I discover.

I need to get the hell out of this room before I lose my goddamn mind.

CHAPTER EIGHT

Paetyn

THE LONGER I SIT ON THE MATTRESS, STARING AT THE MOLDY ROOF, and counting each time the masked man enters the room, the more I begin to lose my goddamn mind. Just as I thought would happen. Each second ticks by painfully slow, leaving me with nothing to do but sit and think. Think about the situation I'm in. Think about my mother and if she's okay. And think about the masked man and the tension between us that only seems to grow each time he visits my room.

A few days have passed since I got myself off to my captor. Shame and guilt have plagued me ever since, reminding me how terrible of a person I am. I have a fiancé searching for me, and here I am finger fucking myself at the thought of another man. The same man who kidnapped me.

I'm beyond fucked up. Or maybe I'm just going crazy the longer I'm trapped inside these four walls. The walls feel as though they're closing in on me, suffocating me inch by inch. If I don't get out of here soon, I'm going to die.

With a huff, I sit up on the mattress, the box springs groaning. Surely, there has to be something in this room that can aid me in getting out of here. I checked the room for a way out when I first woke up, but the masked man entered before I got a good look. Since the warning he issued me about not being able to leave, I haven't snooped around, fear rooting me to the confinement of my bed.

But I'm done sitting around hoping someone will find me and praying that a miracle will descend upon me, allowing me a way to escape. The longer I sit and wait for something positive to happen, the less chance I have of surviving. I refuse to continue being a sitting duck.

I swing my legs over the side of the bed and grip the chain around my ankle to stop it from dragging along the floor. The floorboards beneath my feet groan as I stand. I cringe at the sound, hoping my captor doesn't burst into the room to check what is going on. So, I wait. My lungs scream at me as I hold my breath, waiting to hear his heavy footsteps approach the door.

But nothing happens. No footsteps. No voices. No nothing.

Blowing out a long breath, I get to my knees to search under the bed. There has to be something under here, right? The metal frame has a gap between the base and the floor, with four thin legs holding it upright.

The floor is cold against my chest as I drop to it. My nose crinkles at the assault of dust bunnies, the product of the room being dirty. Who knows when it was last cleaned? But I fight the urge to sneeze and instead hold my breath as I gaze under the bed.

My heart deflates slightly at the empty space shadowed in darkness. Despite my disappointment at there being nothing of substance as far as I can see, I won't allow this to deter me from finding a way out of here.

RESILIENTLY, I REACH UNDER THE BED AND FEEL AROUND, HOPING I CAN latch onto something that can help me. I don't care what it is, at this point. I just need *something*.

Dust continues to find its way into my nose and eyes, making it difficult to keep from coughing or sneezing. But I'm not going to wrap this search up empty-handed. I keep telling myself there has to be—

My eyes round at the feel of metal grazing my fingertips. The thumping of my heart in my ears intensifies at the prospect of having found something useful. I reach forward a fraction more, which allows me to wrap my hand around the mystery object.

I scramble away from the bed, eager to allow my lungs to breathe in fresh air and to see what I found. Falling on my ass, careful not to let the chain scrape against the floor, I eye the item in my hand. To my surprise, it's a metal pole about fifty inches long. It's not super thick, so maybe it had fallen from the bed frame, lying unnoticed beneath it.

The longer I stare at it, turning it over in my hands to ensure I'm not seeing things, the quicker my heart hammers in my chest. This is it. This is what I have been searching for. It may not be enough to help me escape through the boarded up window, but with the right amount of force, if I were to hit my captor over the head with it, I may have enough time to search his body for the key to the lock on the chain around my ankle and find my way out of wherever I'm located.

A smile turns up one side of my mouth as I imagine beating the masked man over the head with the pole, my freedom inches away. I can almost taste fresh air on my tongue and feel sunlight on my skin at the thought of no longer being trapped here.

If this plan is to work, I need to think rationally. The next time he comes into my room to offer me food, I need to wait for that split second when he has his back turned to me before walking over to the chair by the door before I strike. If I'm lucky enough, he won't see it coming.

With newfound confidence coursing through me, I hop onto the bed and sit cross-legged, my eyes focused on the door. I shove the pole under my pillow, my fingertips grazing it slightly as I hold my arms behind my back. Now, all I have to do is wait.

Waiting…

Waiting…

Click.

I eye the door as the lock on the other side is unlatched. Within seconds, the door swings open to reveal the masked man. He enters with the same red tray he uses every time he brings me food. This time, a steaming bowl of chicken and corn soup sits in the middle next to a buttered roll.

Now that he's here, my chance of freedom is so close I can taste it. My nerves kick into overdrive. I watch him intently as he sets the tray on the end of the mattress, stopping briefly to ensure the water bottle doesn't topple over, before he straightens and turns his back to me.

Without hesitation, I grab the pole tightly in my hand and jump from the mattress, ready to clock him over the head with it. As the pole is about to slam into the back of his head, I'm met with a strong arm pressed against my throat, forcing all the air from my lungs.

A GASP BURSTS FROM MY MOUTH WHEN MY BACK HITS SOMETHING HARD —the wall. My chest heaves, begging for air as I struggle against his grip on my throat. The pole slips from my grasp, allowing me to claw at the tattooed arm holding me firmly in place.

"Let go of me, asshole." My voice is strained, but he hears me, nonetheless.

He's in my face now, the mask just as terrifying this close as it is when he sits across the room watching me eat. His chest heaves too, likely with frustration at my attempt to subdue him. A woodsy scent emanates from him, consuming my senses. "What was your plan, little bird? Hm? If you were successful in hitting me with that pathetic excuse for a weapon, what would you have done?"

"I would have got the fuck out of here," I say through wheezes as he slowly cuts off my airway. The thought crosses my mind to lift my leg and kick him straight in the balls, but my head grows fuzzy from the lack of air, making it difficult to think. "You can't keep me here."

The man snorts, a deep sound. It goes straight to my core. "Oh, I plan to keep you here. For as long as I need to. You're not going anywhere."

Despite my inability to breathe, I can't help but wonder what it would feel like for him to touch me elsewhere, leaving goosebumps in his wake. Would he be gentle or ruthless? Would his touch be filled with the same intensity as his eyes whenever they're cast upon me? Would he withhold air from my lungs long enough for me to beg for him to let me breathe, on the brink of passing out, only for him to grant me that permission?

It's embarrassing how turned on I feel right now, especially when the man I was just fantasizing about literally has me on the verge of death.

If I'm going to die, I at least want to see his face. I want to see the man who has held me captive for what feels like at least a week. Even if I were to die right now, my body never to be found, I would be content knowing I saw his face in my final moments. One last 'fuck you' to him.

With what little strength I have left, I reach up and grip the edge of the mask beneath his chin. In one swift movement, I flick it off his head, listening as the plastic connects harshly with the wooden floor.

Wide eyes stare back at me. They're as blue as the deepest part of the ocean where no man has explored. It's what I would imagine I would see if I were to ever drown out in that vast space, begging for help. Even now as I struggle to breathe, the light slipping from my body, I'm lost in the depths of them.

My eyes nearly bulge out of my head when he lets up on my throat. The top of my head feels ready to explode as I cough and splutter, desperate to fill my lungs with air. But he doesn't step away, his grip on my throat still there but not so hard he's cutting off my airway.

Through blurred vision, I take in the features of the man who kidnapped me, and to my utter surprise, he's unlike anything I've ever seen before. He's magnificent, really. Devilishly handsome beyond comprehension with strong facial features, a light dusting of five o'clock shadow, and a jawline that could cut me to the bone. Seeing every part of him all together isn't helping the moisture pooling between my thighs.

Goddamn, what the hell is wrong with me?

He chuckles, the sound vibrating through me to my core. Shaking his head, his soft curls bouncing around his face, he growls, "You shouldn't have done that."

I meet his intense gaze. He has nowhere to hide now that the mask is gone. I can see who he really is, and that could either work in my favor or get me killed.

A slow grin turns up the corners of his mouth as the grip on my throat tightens. Lust and fear tingle across my skin, and I squirm under his grip. If he knows what I'm thinking right now—

A lump lodges itself in my throat when he leans forward, his warm breath fanning against my ear as he whispers, "You're so wet for me, little bird. I can fucking smell it. Tell me, do you like being held captive, hm?"

CHAPTER NINE

Paetyn

MY EYES SNAP OPEN, AND MY HEART THUNDERS IN MY CHEST. I OPEN MY mouth to speak, but only a puff of air escapes, followed by the realization that I'm fucked.

I want to tell him he's insane, but the dampness between my thighs gives me away, calling me a liar. I would rather lose every ounce of air from my lungs before admitting he's right. Hell, I don't even know why my body is reacting to my kidnapper this way, but I'm helpless to stop it. At this point, it has a mind of its own, and apparently, that entails being turned on by being held captive.

Liam's face appears in my mind, reminding me how wrong this is and why I shouldn't be thinking about a stranger the way I am, but when he tightens his grip around my throat, the image disappears, replaced with burning desire deep in my core.

Goddamnit.

"I asked you a question," he utters, his voice dangerously low. He drags his nose across my cheek, his warm breathing smothering my skin as he goes, before he pulls back to meet my gaze. The blue in his irises has darkened, reminding me of the Mariana Trench. With the intensity in which he is looking at me, it feels as though he's holding me over the edge, ready to drown me with one shove.

"I don't want you," I manage to whisper, the words getting lost in the small space between us.

He grins, unfazed by my rejection. "I think you're lying to me."

I gasp when he presses his chest to mine, an obvious bulge present against my sensitive core. My eyes snap shut. I'm unable to look this man in the eye any longer. Shame washes over me like a tidal wave. I shouldn't want this man, but my body is betraying me every step of the way, begging for this stranger to touch me, to put me out of my misery.

The more I try to tell myself I'm only reacting this way because I miss my fiancé's touch, the more I'm starting to realize that maybe my body is reacting this way because the thought of being held captive and taken by a stranger, ignites a foreign emotion in me I didn't know existed. I didn't think I had a kink besides the usual step up from vanilla sex because Liam isn't into that kind of stuff, but it seems this man has unlocked a hidden desire I didn't know I possessed.

"I know you want me to touch you here." He proves his point by dragging his free hand down my chest to rest on my hip. I shiver involuntarily under his touch, but I refuse to look at him.

He hums as he slides his hand up my waist to fiddle with the top button on my shirt. "And here."

My eyes snap open when he uses his free hand to tear my shirt open, the buttons popping free and scattering across the floor. I stare wide-eyed at him, my heart hammering as the fabric falls open, revealing my black lace bra.

He grins at the sight and lowers his hand to the curve of my breast. "Did you wear this just for me, little bird?"

"N-no," I manage to utter through the blood rushing in my ears and the thundering of my heart slamming against my rib cage.

"I think you did. You knew I was watching you." His fingers skim over my sensitive flesh before tugging the cup down, freeing my right breast. I gasp at the cold air hitting my taut nipple. He lifts his eyes to meet mine, a storm brewing within them. "Tell me, did you think about me when you finger-fucked yourself a few days ago, hm? I heard every little sound that came from that sweet mouth."

My back straightens against the wall, my vision blurring. Shit. He heard me? I thought I had been quiet enough that he wouldn't hear me from wherever he was. But it seems he was listening the entire time.

My face burns at the realization.

His large hand cups my breast as his grip around my throat tightens. I fight back a moan at his warm skin against mine, the calluses on his hand brushing against my sensitive nipple.

"It took everything in me to not come in and give you the real deal, but I enjoyed listening to your soft cries and not-so-subtle moans." He rolls his hips forward, brushing his erection over my inflamed core, knocking the air from my lungs. "In fact, I sat on the other side of that door and got myself off to the sound of you because I couldn't help myself."

I gasp, meeting his gaze. "You didn't…"

He smirks as he palms my soft skin, and I force back the moan bubbling up in my throat. "I'm not the type of man who lies to get a reaction out of someone. Every word that comes from my mouth is the truth. So, yes, I did fuck my fist while you fingered your pussy, wishing it was your mouth wrapped around my cock instead."

I swallow hard, unable to form a coherent thought. What's happening right now with his hand around my throat and the other squeezing my breast, and his body pressed against mine while he says such filthy words is jamming every rational thought from reaching the forefront of my mind.

I'm helpless as I stand here, back pressed against the wall and his crotch rubbing mine. I open my mouth to speak, but no sound escapes, just a puff of defeat. My body screams at me to fight back and get this man away from me, but my body doesn't want to cooperate. If anything, it's fighting against my brain to give into his touch, desperate to fuel the fire licking at my sides and growing in my core.

This tug-of-war battle for dominance is slowly tearing me apart, but it's a useless fight when my body arches into his touch, not giving a fuck about what my brain wants. The man grins down at me, palming my skin harder than before.

I know this is wrong, to want a man who kidnapped me, but it's pointless to fight against my instinct to give into my desires.

He lowers his face to meet my gaze, his head tilted to the side. "What's it going to be, little bird?"

My body vibrates with anticipation as I arch my back, pressing my chest to his. I'm unable to speak, so I'm letting my body speak for me. It seems he gets the hint because he releases my throat and breast to grab both of my hands in one of his, slamming them against the wall above my head.

"I fucking knew you were lying." His other hand comes up to caress my cheek before dragging his thumb over my bottom lip. "You want me to fuck you, I can see it in those pretty eyes of yours."

Before I can utter a word, his free hand drops to the button of my jeans, popping it open with ease. His eyes stay on mine as his hand slips between my lace panties and inflamed skin. When his fingers find my soaked core, arousal ruining my underwear, he grins as his fingers drag between the folds.

All he fucking does is grin.

I throw my head back against the wall when he plunges two fingers inside, foregoing the foreplay. My hips roll forward, meeting his thrusts. Each time his thick fingers drag against my walls, bringing with it a wave of pleasure, I'm unable to stop the moans falling from my mouth.

I hate that I'm enjoying this because I know I shouldn't, but the boat of rational thinking has long since left the dock, leaving me stranded and helpless.

"You're so fucking wet for me, little bird," he murmurs as he continues to pound his fingers into me, the rhythm almost punishing. "Your cunt is begging for more, and luckily for you, I'm in a giving mood right now."

He removes his hand from me at lightning speed and releases his hold of my wrists. My heart hammers in my throat as he steps back, but only to give him space to shove my jeans down my legs. He gestures for me to step out of them.

When I'm essentially naked in front of him, save for my ruined shirt, tugged down bra, and underwear, he points to the bed. "Get on your knees for me. I want to see that ass."

Jesus. His words are filthier than anything Liam has ever said to me, and somehow, it makes me wetter than I already am.

I exhale a soft sigh and do as instructed. My legs shake beneath me as I kneel on the bed. His presence behind me looms like an impending storm cloud ready to cause havoc. Anticipation gnaws at my side, sending jolts of electricity to my fingertips.

"I said, show me that ass, little bird."

His hand on the back of neck forcing me forward until I'm on my hands startles a surprised gasp from my lips. With my ass in the air, he hums in admiration.

"So fucking round and perfect." His hand comes down on my right cheek, and I moan in response. "And it's all mine."

I want to tell him that's not true, but I'm momentarily distracted by him shoving my underwear down to my bent knees. He drops to his knees behind me as his hands roam over my backside, touching me as if he can't get enough.

My forehead meets the sheets beneath me as I focus on my breathing and not the pounding of my heart against my rib cage. Every touch from this man has me seeing stars, my body reacting without hesitation. If I were to touch my skin where his hands have been, I would be burned because, right now, I feel like I'm on fire.

He drags a finger up between my thighs, circling my drenched clit. I groan into the mattress, unable to stop myself.

"You're making a mess of yourself, little bird. So wet and needy."

His lips make contact with my pussy, and I just about lose my vision. I grip the sheets and groan as his tongue slips between my folds, sucking and licking like a starved man out in the forest. His large hands grip my ass, holding me in place as he fucking devours me.

"Shit," I hiss, my vision blurring as his tongue punches in and out of me. "God."

"I can be your god," he murmurs against my lips, the vibration sending another moan out of my throat. "All you have to do is ask."

Just as his tongue slides between my folds again, his fingers digging painfully into my skin, he's gone. I'm all but panting as I hear what sounds like a belt buckle being loosened behind me. I look over my shoulder to see him pulling his belt through the loops of his pants, dropping it haphazardly to the floor beside him.

My eyes widen when he unbuttons his jeans and shoves them down. Within seconds, his thick cock springs free. Angry veins circle the base like vines, the size of it intimidating. It's by far the biggest I've ever seen.

"You like what you see, little bird?" he utters as he catches my gaze.

I swallow, unable to speak. How do I respond to something like that? *No, I'm actually terrified of you putting that massive thing anywhere near me.* But that's not true. Yes, I like it.

He steps behind me, his hand grazing over the curve of my ass before slapping it with such force I nearly drop to my stomach. "I asked you a question."

"Ye-yes," I murmur, throat thick.

"Good girl." His finger slides between my aching folds, gathering my arousal before using the same hand to pump his cock, all the while his gaze holds mine.

Goddamn.

Although he's fully clothed, I can't deny how sexy he is. This man is unlike anyone I've ever seen, his beauty unmatched. Just the sight of him watching me from behind messy strands of inky hair tightens the tension building in my core.

I gasp when the crown brushes against my entrance. My fingers grip the sheets tighter, partly to stop my arms from trembling but also to hold me in place as he nudges inside of me, inch by painfully slow inch.

"Fuck," he groans as his hands find my hips, fingers digging into the raw skin again. "You're so fucking tight."

I'm breathless by the time he bottoms out, the size of him intruding and overwhelming. My body is vibrating as I adjust to his size, the fullness slowly morphing into pleasure.

His hand comes down on my ass, the sound echoing around the empty room. He pulls back, only to slam into me again. I gasp, having not expected him to do that and hold onto the sheets for dear life as he continues to draw back and slam into me at a rhythm that has my head spinning and my eyes rolling back into my head.

"That's it," he grunts as his grip on my hips tighten. "You take my cock so well."

I respond with a moan as his thighs meet mine in a symphony of slaps. His hand wraps around my throat, pulling my head back and my chest forward as he continues to drive into me, unrelenting. His grip isn't tight enough to constrict my airways, but it's enough that my vision blurs at the edges. It's a pleasure I have never experienced before but something I find myself enjoying.

A deep, guttural groan falls from his lips the deeper he hits inside me, as if he can't get enough and needs more. He strikes me as the type of man who is far from vanilla, possibly into some crazy shit, so he needs that something extra to get him off. What though, I'm not sure.

My palms are slick with sweat as he fucks me like a mad man, our breathing mixing in whirlwind of pleasure and ecstasy. I'm unable to form a single sound that isn't a moan, and profanities fall from his lips every so often, tightening the tension building in my core.

My lungs ache for air as he continues to hold my throat, and my legs and back are screaming at me to relieve the pressure he's putting on them, but I don't want this to end. The pleasure and desire coursing through every inch of my body is unlike anything I've ever felt. Being with this man is intense and fucking crazy, but I crave more. Something, anything. Just *more*.

As if hearing my thoughts, he releases my throat and pulls out of me. A whine slips past my lips at his absence, but it doesn't last long before he grabs my waist and flips me on my back. Our eyes clash in a fiery blaze as he stands above me, his breathing erratic. A light sheen of sweat covers the inky strands of hair and causes them to stick to his forehead.

My panties torn, it's easy for him to grab my knees and force them apart, allowing him to step between them. Without tearing his eyes from me, he grabs the base of his cock and shoves into me. I throw my head back as another moan filters into the air.

The bed is high enough that it allows him the perfect angle to drive into me relentlessly. My tits bounce wildly with each thrust, and I struggle to force air into my lungs as my core tightens, chasing a release.

I wish he wasn't clothed so I could see what's hidden beneath. Having me naked and completely at his mercy while keeping his clothes on is likely his way of staying in control of the situation and keeping that distance between us. Because at the end of the day, this is just sex and nothing more. At least, that's what I'm telling myself.

"You're so fucking beautiful," he murmurs more to himself as his eyes roam over my body. His finger drags against my bottom lip, lingering for a moment before pulling away. "It's a shame I don't kiss and tell because I want to claim those fucking lips."

Before I can ask what he means by that, he pulls out to the tip before slamming back into me, distracting me from my previous thoughts. The pressure building in my core is reaching a breaking point, and I'm about ready to lose my mind.

"Come for me, little bird," he grunts, his voice dangerously low. "Now."

And that's all it takes for me to explode, the orgasm so intense my body trembles and my mind goes blank. A scream erupts from my throat as electricity races through my veins, and heat explodes in my core. If I didn't know any better, I would say it feels like I'm dying, but I know that's not the case. I'm very much alive, and he's very much pounding into me like a mad man as I ride out the intensity.

Moments later, he growls before pulling out and spilling onto my stomach. I gasp as his hot seed coats my skin in a splatter of white.

"Holy fuck," he breathes as he pumps his cock, working through his own orgasm.

Holy fuck, indeed.

"Oh, my God." I'm at a loss for words as I stare at my stomach, the realization of what just happened slowly dawning on me. "Oh, my *God.*"

He releases a low breath as he stands to his full height, shoves his cock back into his pants, zips them, and smiles down at me. He doesn't say anything as he wraps his arm around my waist and pulls me to my feet.

My legs are wobbly as he guides me to the attached bathroom and sits me on the edge of the cold sink. I'm still in a daze as I watch him grab the hand towel and wipe my stomach clean, the gesture gentle after the beast I just saw.

"When this is all over, little bird, I will find you."

My brows dip into a frown, and I open my mouth to ask what he means by that, but the words die on my tongue as I stare at him. Intense blue eyes gaze back at me, filled with the silence of a promise of making good on his words.

The thundering of my heart drowns out the blood rushing in my ears and the ice filling my veins.

What the hell have I just gotten myself into?

CHAPTER TEN

Paetyn

BANG!

My eyes snap open at the loud noise. It's hard to figure out where it came from within the house, but it sounded close. I'm disoriented with sleep-crusted eyes as I pull the thin sheet up to my chin, staring at the locked door to the room.

What is my kidnapper doing? Besides the time he woke me up talking loudly on the phone, I tend not to hear a peep from him throughout the day. I don't know what he does when he isn't bringing me food and watching me eat—or fucking me like a depraved man—but he certainly doesn't usually make noise like that.

My heart nearly leaps out of my throat at the sound of rushing footsteps. Not just one set of footsteps, but I detect multiple.

What is going on? Has my captor finally decided to sell me to a group of traffickers, and now they've come to collect me?

I scoot back further on the mattress, the box springs squeaking, mixing with the panic building in my chest. Fear nips at my fingers as a million and one scenarios race through my mind at lightning speed of what could become of me when those footsteps reach the door.

What will happen when the door flies open? I have no doubt my life will change forever, but in what way?

I don't hear the lock unlatch from the outside before the door swings open, slamming against the wall behind it with a violent bang. But I don't see the masked man rush into the room. No, it's a man wearing a SWAT uniform, his handgun trained directly at me.

His eyes find mine across the room. Time feels as though it has slowed down as we stare at each other, neither of us moving an inch. Two other men dressed in the same type of uniform file into the room, their guns trained at me, too.

Despite having three guns pointed at me, relief washes through my veins. I relax against the headboard and exhale the breath I had been holding.

The first man who entered nods at me. Most of his head is covered by a helmet, but his deep brown eyes find mine. "Are you Paetyn Jones?"

My head spins with adrenaline and relief as I stare back at them. I open my mouth to speak, but all that comes out is a breathy, "Yes, I am."

They lower their guns at my admission. The two men who arrived after the first step out of the room, one already speaking into a walkie-talkie. The first man steps forward, slipping his gun back into the holster on his waist. "You're going to be okay, miss. We're going to get you to safety."

Warmth fills my chest, and for the first time in seven days, excitement floods my veins. I can't wait to get out of this place. I throw the sheet off my body, ready to tell the officer about the chain around my ankle, but to my surprise, the chain is nowhere to be seen. The skin where it once entrapped me is blistering slightly and bruised, but it's otherwise free.

Huh… when did the masked man have time to take it off? When he left me last night, thoroughly exhausted, the chain had still been attached to me.

Now that I think about it, where is he right now?

"Let's go, miss. We need to get you checked out." The officer extends his hand to me, and I take it, allowing him to help me off the bed. After he cleaned me up last night, my kidnapper provided me with a clean T-shirt. I'm wearing that, my bra, and my jeans. I have no idea what happened to my ruined panties.

Maybe he kept them as a souvenir.

"Where is he?" I murmur, looking around the room I have been trapped in for seven days. "Did you find him?"

"The man who kidnapped you?" the officer questions as he guides me out of the room. "No, we haven't been able to locate him as of yet. But rest assured, we have our best men on the job. We will find him. From what we have surveyed of the area, whoever kidnapped you left no evidence behind. This leads us to believe he was a professional."

A professional? Why would a professional kidnapper go through all this trouble to kidnap me, keep me trapped here for seven days, and then suddenly disappear without so much as getting a dollar for me?

He got nothing from me at all—besides my dignity after last night, of course.

None of this makes any sense.

We step into the hallway I had heard my captor walk down three times a day for the past week. As we walk down it, the floorboards creaking beneath us, I realize it's not as long as I thought it was. Or maybe that was just my imagination tricking me into thinking the house was larger than it is. In reality, I have been staying in a shack.

The hallway opens into what appears to be a small living area with an attached kitchen, a single couch, and a tiny television on a wooden table. No artwork hanging on the beige walls, the kitchen cabinets and appliances have seen better days, and the cushions on the couch have holes and burn marks scattered across them. There isn't much to the small space, and as I walk toward the front door, I realize the room I was trapped in was the only bedroom.

Had the masked man been sleeping on the couch this whole time?

The moment I walk through the front door, sunlight assaults my vision. I hiss at the intrusion and cover my eyes. As much as I've dreamed about feeling the warm sunlight on my skin, I wasn't expecting how much it would hurt seeing it for the first time in seven days. But I don't let it deter me from gazing around at my surroundings.

Trees as far as the eye can see surround me in every direction. No matter which way I turn, thick green foliage meets my gaze. It doesn't feel like I'm anywhere close to New York City, so where the hell am I?

"Come on, miss. We have someone waiting to see you."

I follow the officer over to the multiple SWAT vehicles parked among the tree line nearby. It's hard to make sense of the number of officers lingering around, talking on their phones or to each other. About what? I'm not sure. Maybe they're discussing where my captor went and how best to find his ass.

A head of dirty blond hair catches my eye before I see his face. Liam turns away from the officer he's talking to and meets my gaze. A smile splits his face at the sight of me, and I must admit I do the same.

I never thought I would see my fiancé again, and now that I'm looking at him, a wave of emotions crashes over me.

He's here. Liam is really here.

He rushes in my direction, and as soon as his arms wrap around me in a tight embrace, I'm unable to stop the waterworks. Tears stream down my face as he brushes his hand over my hair, soothing me. This is the physical touch I have been craving.

"Oh, Pae, I'm so glad you're okay," Liam murmurs against my hair, his arms tightening around me.

I bury my face in his chest, inhaling his familiar scent. Tears continue to moisten my cheeks as I sob into his white button-down shirt. I'm creating a mess, I know, but I'm helpless to stop it. My emotions are all over the place. Guilt is one of them, reminding me of my betrayal of Liam last night, but I push the feeling away, not wanting to think about it.

"You're okay," Liam coos, rubbing my back with his other hand. "I've got you. You're safe now."

Blinking away the tears, I lift my head to meet his gray eyes. "How did they find me?"

"When Raya called to tell me what happened the night you were kidnapped, I went straight to the police to help in any way I could. I provided them with as much information as possible that could be used to track you down. We have spent every waking moment the past seven days trying to locate you, and after we got wind from an informant in prison about a young woman being held captive out in the forest outside of the city, we knew we had found you."

Through my blurred vision, the warmth in Liam's eyes calms my racing heart, and the tears slow. Being in his arms still doesn't feel real, but I know now I'm safe. I'm free of my captor, and hopefully, I never have to see his face again.

"You saved me," I breathe. Knowing Liam had a hand in my rescue swells my heart with pride and love. He did everything he could to help me, and I'll be forever grateful for his dedication. All those nights I laid awake wondering what he was doing, and if he was looking for me, weren't for nothing. "I love you."

Liam smiles and leans down to press a delicate kiss to my forehead, nearly bringing more tears to my eyes. "I love you too, Pae. Now, let's go get you checked out. The further we are from this place, the better. From now on, you'll always be safe with me."

Liam wraps his arm around my shoulders, holding me to his side as he guides me over to the ambulance nearby. The further I get from the shack, the stronger the memories become of what occurred while I was trapped inside. No matter how hard I push them to the back of my mind, they continue to claw their way to the surface, making their presence known. They refuse to allow me to forget—to move on.

I manage to smile at the kind nurse waiting to look me over, but I'm lost once again in the deepest part of the ocean, slowly drowning but unable to scream for help.

CHAPTER ELEVEN

Paetyn

THE INSISTENT BEEPING OF THE MACHINES SURROUNDING MY BED HAS been driving me insane all night. At this point, I would rather have the silence of the shack I spent the last week trapped in.

Since arriving at the hospital yesterday afternoon, I haven't slept a wink. It's a little hard when nurses and doctors are rushing in and out of the room to check my vitals and ensure I'm doing okay. Add to that a horde of reporters trying to get a statement from the woman who survived a kidnapping and lived to tell the tale and you've got yourself a goddamn nightmare.

Thankfully, Liam has been kind enough to handle the media for me as I'm in no condition to be speaking with them. I'm exhausted, desperate for a proper night's rest in my bed at home, and want nothing more than to see my mother. When I was rescued, Liam informed me that he had been visiting my mother to ensure she knew he was doing everything he could to find me. I was grateful to hear such an update since I had been worried about her the entire time I was gone.

But now, I get to see her for myself. The nurses permitted me to go visit her, but only for twenty minutes so I don't overexert myself. No matter how many times I tell them I'm fine, they insist on me resting. Liam helps me slip into a robe so that I am covered in the skimpy hospital gown, and we head off for a visit.

The elevator doors ding open, and Liam and I step inside. His hand rests firmly on my lower back as we stand side by side, watching the elevator doors close. He managed to get away from the reporters long enough to accompany me to visit my mom.

"Thanks for coming with me," I murmur.

Liam leans over and plants a soft kiss on the top of my head. "Of course. I know how worried you are about her. Being away from her for this long couldn't have been easy."

"It wasn't," I admit quietly. "I spent many nights lying awake wondering if she was okay or not."

"She was in good hands, I promise." Liam pulls me to his side. "But you don't have to worry any longer, okay? I will continue to ensure she gets the best possible treatment."

The elevator doors ding open, revealing the hustle and bustle of nurses rushing around. Liam gestures for me to walk first, so I do. We walk down the hallway to the ward where my mom is located. When we approach the front desk, the small television hanging on the wall behind them broadcasts the news. And, of course, my face is plastered across it, alongside Liam's.

"Liam Aster, the well-known Senator running for reelection, has worked tirelessly the last seven days to track down his missing fiancée, Paetyn Jones, after she was kidnapped by an unknown male. After many sleepless nights, Mr. Aster helped the police locate Miss Jones outside the city in a shack hidden in the forest. Miss Jones was found unharmed. The police are still on the hunt for her kidnapper, so if you saw something suspicious last Friday night in the downtown area, then you are urged to share the information with the police."

I sigh. The media coverage about my kidnapping is never-ending. I fear what it'll be like when I do get to leave tomorrow morning. From what Liam has told me, reporters have been set up on our front lawn for the past 24 hours, waiting for me to return. The thought of coming home after being away for so long and seeing so many people waiting for me makes my chest tighten.

"Come on, Pae." Liam presses a kiss to the top of my head, leading me away from the front desk. "Just ignore the news, okay? I'm sure, in a few days, it'll all blow over, and they'll find a new story to be obsessed with."

"You're right," I hum softly, licking my lips. "Thank you for taking care of it for me. It's not something I'm up to facing just yet."

"It's my pleasure, Pae. Anything for you."

My mother's room comes into view at the end of the hallway. The uncomfortable feeling in my chest from seeing the news just now dissipates at the thought of seeing her. It's been far too long. I just hope she's doing okay.

When we enter the room, Mom is sitting up in bed, her eyes focused on the television playing a trashy reality TV show. The corner of her mouth is turned up in a half smile as she picks at the leftover lunch food on the table beside her.

"Mom," I breathe. I'm unable to keep tears from lining my bottom lashes at the sight of her. Although it's only been about ten days since I've seen her, the skin in her cheeks looks a little more hollow, likely from the chemo treatment. Despite her skin being paler than usual, the brightness of her eyes hasn't changed.

I almost burst into sobs when she looks at me.

Tears well in her eyes as realization washes over her features. "Pae? Is that you?"

I step away from Liam and rush to her side, wrapping my arms around her neck so tightly I fear I may cut off her airway. Her shoulders are thinner, an indication she has lost weight. The floral scent clinging to her skin makes me smile against her neck, forcing the tears to flow freely down my cheeks.

This moment right here is what I dreamed about every night before I went to sleep while in captivity. My mom is the most important person in my life, so I'm glad to be back in her arms. And I have

Liam to thank for that. Without his help, I may never have gotten out of that shack alive.

"Where have you been, sweetie?" Mom asks gently, her voice smooth. "Liam told me you had been kidnapped, but I learned on the news yesterday they found you."

I sniffle back tears and tighten my embrace. "I'm okay, Mom. I promise. The doctors just didn't think I was strong enough to come see you yet, but I'm fine."

We pull away from each other, and I lean into Mom's touch as she caresses my cheek. She smiles up at me, tears brimming her own eyes. "What happened to you?"

"I can't talk about it too much as it's an open investigation, but just know I'm okay. The man who took me… he didn't hurt me."

Mom blows out a shaky breath and drops her hand from my cheek to hold my hand tightly. "I suppose I have your wonderful fiancé here to thank. He told me all about the hard work he had been putting in with the police to find you."

I cast a glance over my shoulder at where Liam stands by the closed door, his hands shoved into the pockets of his black slacks. He lifts a shoulder in response, a warm smile on his lips.

"If it wasn't for him, I'm not sure I would be here right now."

"I can't take all the credit," Liam says. He walks forward to stand beside me, his hand coming up to rest firmly on my lower back. "All I did was aid the police in finding Pae by offering information on her last known whereabouts and whatnot. Once they managed to gain access to the local cameras around her office, it was easy sailing from there."

"But still," Mom says, warmth in her tone, "you helped find my baby girl, and for that, I'm eternally grateful."

Liam grins. "Thank you, Ms. Jones. I would do anything for Pae."

I pat her hand covering mine and smile. "Okay, enough about me. I want to hear what you've been up to since I've been gone."

Mom is hesitant to change the subject from me to her, given everything I've been through, but I'm tired of having the spotlight trained only on me. I'm not anyone of importance, besides being the fiancée of a politician, so I don't feel it necessary to have everyone around me focused on my situation.

Instead, I would rather listen to my mom tell me about her treatment—which we can only afford thanks to Liam continuing to pay for her medical bills—what she has been watching on TV lately, and how she feels given her diagnosis.

But as she tells me everything I want to hear, I find myself getting lost in thought. It's unintentional, but I can't help it.

The man who kidnapped me has been plaguing my mind ever since I was rescued. Thoughts of him make themselves known at unexpected times, and no matter how hard I try to force them from my thoughts, they come right back. The way he touched me, licked me… God, it's been driving me insane.

Where is he right now? Has he been caught?

I shouldn't care whether he's dead or alive, but my body refuses to allow him to leave my subconscious. Instead, he's been firmly planted in a small corner of my mind, refusing to leave. I wish I could forget about him because I know it's wrong to think about the man who kidnapped me that I betrayed my fiancé with.

It's not beyond me how fucked up the situation is.

But as Liam listens intently to my mom speak about the TV show she's watching currently, the same women's perfume I've smelled countless times on my fiancé's collar wafts around me like a storm cloud. And for a brief moment, I wonder just how worried he was about me the past seven days.

CHAPTER TWELVE

Paetyn

UTENSILS CLINGING AGAINST PORCELAIN PLATES ECHO IN THE BACK OF my mind. It's a sound that wouldn't normally annoy me, but when it's mixed with Liam and his father's nonstop chattering about politics and how Liam is doing in the polls, it's now irritating the hell out of me.

I sigh. I've only taken two bites out of my medium-rare steak, though it is cooked to perfection, and I haven't touched the roasted veggies beside it. I haven't been able to eat much since I've gotten home. I don't know if I got used to eating sandwiches and soup while being held in the shack or if my lack of appetite is due to my mind constantly thinking about that damn masked man.

Either way, Liam's mom is starting to notice my full plate compared to theirs.

"Paetyn, honey. Are you okay?"

I lift my eyes from the cold food and meet Angie's gaze. Her light blue eyes hold a quizzical look about them as they search my face. Angie lowers her cutlery beside her empty plate and clasps her fingers together on her lap. She is the epitome of class with her diamond jewelry, ironed beige blouse, and black chinos tailored to fit her frame. Not a strand of blonde hair is out of place from the styled up-do.

In one word, she's beautiful, but I suppose that's what money can buy you.

I clear my throat and force a smile on my face, but it doesn't reach my eyes. It never does when I speak with Liam's mother. "I'm okay, Angie. Just tired."

Liam and his father, Pat, are still conversing across the dining table, neither of them stopping to take a breath and listen in on our conversation. I mean, there isn't much to listen to, but I know I'm tired of hearing about what politician is doing what and who is tanking in the polls.

"Well, that would explain your lack of appetite," Angie comments, her lips set into a thin line. "Unless the chefs did a terrible job of cooking your meal."

I shake my head. The last thing I need is for one of their many chefs to get in trouble for something they didn't do. "The food is fantastic, really. I've just had a long week, as you can imagine, and it seems the exhaustion is creeping up on me."

There is no way in hell I'm going to mention my inability to forget about the masked man and the things he did to me. The way he touched me; his eyes peering into mine as if I were the only woman in the world. Or the way he told me he would find me. His tone wasn't threatening, but it was a promise. A promise that sent a shiver down my spine and heated my core to almost boiling temperatures.

And when I have a fiancé, thinking about another man fucking me is the last thing I should be doing. I know I should forget it ever happened, like water under the bridge, but I still feel the ghost of his fingers grazing my skin when I lay awake at night, staring at the ceiling and listening to Liam snore beside me.

No matter how many times I tell myself it's wrong to think about him, I can't stop. And I have no idea why. Maybe it's Stockholm Syndrome, or maybe I'm just fucked up.

As a psychologist, you would think I would understand what's going on in my brain, but the truth is, I'm beyond clueless, and it's driving me insane. It's enough to make me not want to eat anything.

"Good," Angie responds, breaking me from my thoughts. "If you're not feeling well, I will make sure the chefs don't bring a plate of dessert for you. The last thing you need is to upset your stomach." She raises a perfectly shaped brow at me and leans across the table. "I mean, unless you're… you know what…"

I nearly choke on my saliva. No way she is insinuating what I think she is…

"Mom," Liam cuts in from beside me, stealing his mother's attention away from me. "Pae isn't pregnant. If she was, you would know." Well, at least he heard that part of our conversation.

Angie clicks her tongue and leans back in her chair, turning to regard her son. "I would hope so. If my future daughter-in-law is pregnant, I want to be the first to know about it."

It's on the tip of my tongue to say, *My mother would be the first to know*, but I grit my teeth to keep the words from tumbling out. Liam doesn't seem to notice my clenched jaw as he looks between his parents. He's dressed just as nicely as them in a black two-piece suit, matching Pat's. Like father, like son.

Liam rubs the back of his neck. "Can we change the subject, please?"

"Yes, let's do that." Pat shifts on his chair and focuses his attention on me. His gray eyes are more intense than Liam's, and I can't help but shrink a little under his gaze. "How has it been going back to work, Paetyn? I'm sure it's been a lot to adjust to."

After I was released from the hospital, about two days after I was rescued, I spent one day resting before I told Liam I had to get out of the house. Not only were my memories of the masked man consuming every waking moment, but the reporters on the front lawn were a nightmare to deal with. Every time I stepped foot outside, they were right there to snap a photo and throw multiple questions at me. I felt like a zoo animal, gazing around in stunned silence.

I knew if I stayed in the house for a second longer, I would lose my mind. Well, more than I already have.

"I was happy to be back," I answer, fiddling with the silver engagement ring on my left hand. The diamond in the center is far larger than I would choose for myself, but Liam insisted it be that big so everyone around me knew I was taken. "My clients were very understanding about my absence, which I was grateful for. But now I'm playing catch up with rescheduled appointments while sticking to my normal schedule. It's a lot of work, but I'm enjoying the distraction."

"Good, good," Pat says, nodding his head. Although, by the way his eyes shift from me to Liam, I know he doesn't care in the slightest what I'm up to. I might be marrying his son, but he has zero interest in my life. "I'm sure you've heard the good news about Liam."

The corner of my mouth twitches as I slip a tight smile onto my face. "Yeah, he told me all about how well he's doing in the polls against his opponent. I'm sure his popularity will only gain with his next rally."

Liam rests his hand on my thigh, squeezing gently. "I couldn't have done it without you by my side, Pae. Your love and support is what gets me through each day."

"The news of your kidnapping and Liam's part in rescuing you certainly helped," Angie chimes in. She dabs her mouth with the thick cloth napkin on her lap, her lips set into a thin line.

Silence settles over the table as I stare at her, too stunned to speak. Liam coughs awkwardly beside me, his hand still resting on my thigh. "Mom, that's not really appropriate to say one week after Pae was brought home."

Angie shrugs, not an ounce of shame on her aged face. Money has certainly bought her some Botox over the years, smoothing out most of her wrinkles. "I'm just saying, honey."

I blow out a long breath and put my napkin on the table next to my plate. Although anger bubbles in my veins at Angie's implication that Liam is gaining popularity in the polls because he helped rescue me from my kidnapper, I can't let them know they've rattled me. I don't want to make a fool of myself in front of Liam's parents by speaking my mind or putting Liam in a difficult situation.

Instead, I stand and smile. Nothing about the gesture is genuine. "If you'll excuse me, I'm going to step outside to get some fresh air."

Liam grabs my hand, his palm slightly sweaty against my skin. "Are you okay?"

"I'll be fine," I answer. "I'll be back soon."

I feel their eyes on me as I walk away from the table but make no move to stop or look back. When I step into the brightly lit hallway, I exhale a long breath. My heart races in my chest as I continue walking. The pristine white walls feel as though they're closing in on me, but I manage to reach the front door.

The air is cool against the exposed skin of my arms, but I welcome it. Anything to distract me from the disaster of a dinner I've been sitting through or the masked man taking up far too much space in my mind.

My black heels click against the wooden boards on the porch as I walk to the large swing. As I take a seat, I close my eyes and focus on my breathing. I wasn't lying when I said I needed to get some fresh air. If I sat in that room any longer, I fear my head may have exploded across the room.

I have never liked visiting Liam's parents for family dinners each week because they mostly consisted of me listening to them talk politics and answering the same questions about work. The wedding planning comes up quite a lot, but it's a tired topic at this point. I would rather they ask me questions about my interests or my goals and dreams for my future with their son.

The Aster family live in their own wealthy world where they have zero interest in getting to know anyone they consider beneath them —including me. It makes it hard to connect with them, but over the years that I've known them, I've come to the conclusion that it's best I be civil instead of trying to get into their good graces. As long as they approve of me being with Liam, I won't have any problems.

Well, as far as I know.

I sigh and open my eyes, gazing up at the stars twinkling high in the sky. It's peaceful out here. With the house being on a piece of property outside of New York City, it provides a sense of calmness one can't find in the city. It's one of the main reasons why I tolerate these family dinners.

My phone dings in my lap, disrupting the serene feeling of sitting alone among the stars. It's likely Raya checking in on me again. She visited me while I was in the hospital, but work has been crazy this past week, so we haven't had a chance to catch up yet. When we finally do get the chance to catch up, especially because we didn't get a chance to before I was kidnapped, I'm sure we'll be talking for hours. But I'm not mad about it.

The light from my phone screen is nearly blinding in the depths of the darkness swirling around me. When my eyes adjust to the light, my heart stops beating in my chest as I read the words on the screen.

UNKNOWN: *Found you, little bird.*

With trembling hands, I lower my phone and stare ahead at the vast darkness before me. Nothing but trees line the property, keeping it somewhat hidden from the rest of civilization.

So, how the hell did the masked man find me? I know it's him because he's the only person who calls me 'little bird.'

The longer I stare out into the darkness, my heart non-existent in my chest, I kid myself into thinking I feel a pair of ocean blue eyes staring back at me. I know that isn't possible given the security lining the property, but it still doesn't stop my mind from free falling once again into the depths of the ocean which has plagued my mind the past week.

If he has found me, what does he plan to do with me?

And will I like it?

CHAPTER THIRTEEN

Paetyn

"Okay, that's it for our session, Amy. I will see you again in two weeks."

My patient stands from the chair opposite me, fiddling with the ends of her long, auburn hair. "Thank you for today."

I lean forward to lay my notebook on the wooden coffee table in front of me and stand, meeting Amy's gaze. A warm smile touches my lips as I regard her. She has been coming to see me regularly for the past two years. She's in her early twenties, struggling with debilitating anxiety and depression. Despite being diagnosed with something life-altering, she still makes the effort every two weeks to sit down and talk with me. Amy might not see it yet, but in the time I have been seeing her, she has made progress. Mostly in the way she thinks and some of her actions. But there is still much more progress to make.

"Get home safe, okay?" I wait for Amy to pass me before I follow her out of the room. My heels click against the vinyl floor, echoing throughout the front foyer.

Clarissa smiles at me from behind the computer monitor as we pass by. Once again, she is working late. I need to remind her it's okay to leave work on time. Life is too short to be bogged down by a job.

Maybe I'm saying this because of my recent kidnapping, but still, life really is too short.

Before Amy steps through the door, she turns to face me, her pale brown eyes wide. "I'm glad you're okay, after... you know. I was worried about you when I heard about your disappearance."

Oh, if only she knew how messed up my head has been this past week. But I can't tell my client that sort of information. Instead, I offer a warm smile. "Thank you for your concern, Amy. I'm okay."

The corner of her lips turn up in a smile and she nods. "Have a good night."

"You too."

The door closes behind her with a soft click, and I'm quick to push the lock into place. I'm ready to get home and find something to take my mind off everything that has happened the past week since I was recused.

After the text message I got last night from the masked man... I need something to distract me from the meaning behind it.

"Paetyn," Clarissa calls from the front desk. "Are you okay?"

I clear my throat and step away from the door. A smile slips onto my lips as I straighten the dark brown cardigan wrapped tightly around my shoulders. "I'm fine, just tired. It's been a long day of back to back sessions."

Clarissa's brown eyes flash with sympathy as I approach her. "Go home and get some rest, okay?"

"You should take your own advice," I respond with a small smile. "I mean it. You work too hard. Take the night off, and go out with your boyfriend. It's Friday night, after all."

Clarissa blows out a long breath, running her fingers through the ends of her blonde hair. "Yeah, you're right. I'm just about done with the work for today anyway."

"That's the spirit." I step away from the desk and walk toward my office. "I'll see you on Monday."

Once I have my belongings and lock my office, I bid farewell to a few other people in the office and step onto the streets of New York City. The air is cold against the bare skin of my cheeks. But thankfully, I don't have to walk to the parking lot I would normally park in because Liam has insisted I have a driver take me to and from work each day. He doesn't feel comfortable with me driving myself and having to walk alone at night after what happened.

I must admit, I feel the same. That's why I didn't put up a fight, and allow Liam to hire a driver.

Toby, said driver, nods at me from his position in front of the passenger door. When I approach him, he opens the door to the black Rolls Royce. "Good evening, Miss Jones."

"Hi, Toby," I say softly, sliding into the car. "Thank you."

I watch the middle-aged man with graying hair round the front of the vehicle. He slides into the front seat effortlessly, wasting no time switching the ignition on and pulling out to merge with the traffic.

With it being a Friday night, we're stuck in bumper to bumper traffic. Everyone is keen to get home and relax. Angry honks and annoyed voices shouting throughout the street hit my ears, but I ignore them. My mind feels numb as I stare straight ahead, staring at the back of the yellow taxi inches from the front of the car.

My phone vibrates in my lap. I snap my eyes downward to see a text message from Raya on the screen.

RAYA: Let's meet up for dinner tonight. Since you've been out of hospital, I've barely seen you. I miss you, Pae.

I drag my bottom lip between my teeth as I read my best friend's message. She's right. Between getting back to work and avoiding the media, I haven't had the chance to sit down with her and catch up properly. Liam has been adamant that I stay at home and rest after work, but I'm in desperate need of some girl time.

Meeting up with Raya is just the distraction I need.

PAETYN: Absolutely! Text me the details of where to meet, and I'll be there as soon as I can.

I lift my phone to my ear after dialing Liam's number. It's best I let him know right away about my changed plans so he's not worried about my whereabouts. He's been busy at work this past week with his campaign, so there is a chance he may not answer.

When I reach his message bank, his voice filtering through my ears, I bite my lip. I leave him a message, detailing my plans to meet up with Raya. I hope he's not annoyed I'm going out tonight, but I'm not going to be in any danger. Not when I'm with another person, and I'll have Toby outside the restaurant if I need him.

I drop my phone in my lap and turn to Toby. His gaze is focused ahead at the traffic, but I know he's watching me from the corner of his eye. "Toby, change of plans. I need you to drive me somewhere else."

He nods. "As you wish, Miss Jones."

* * *

The Mexican restaurant Raya asked me to meet her at is busy. Loud voices ring throughout the cramped space, and my vision blurs at the edges, mixing with the burnt orange walls and bright yellow tablecloths.

I inhale a deep breath and push my way through the restaurant, clutching my handbag to my side. Fried beans and guacamole waft through the air, making my stomach growl. I hadn't realized how hungry I was until I stepped inside, surrounded by delicious food and endless glasses of frozen margaritas.

A head of strawberry blonde hair falls into my line of sight. My mouth turns up into a half smile when I lock eyes with Raya, her golden irises, with flecks of green, push away the tension in my shoulders.

God, I have missed my best friend.

"Pae!" she calls out, standing. "Over here."

I smile and push my way through the last little bit of space, making sure to apologize for bumping shoulders with one of the workers. As soon as I reach the table, Raya wraps her arms around my neck, holding me close to her body. My eyes flutter close as the scent of her lotus and vanilla shampoo fills my senses.

Warmth spreads through my chest. I dreamed about hugging my best friend while I was held captive. Tears threaten to form in the corner of my eyes, but I blink them away.

"I've missed you so much," Raya murmurs, her grip around me tightening.

"I've missed you too." My words are breathless as Raya squeezes the air out of my lungs, but I welcome it. Having her arms around me is better than lying on a dingy bed wondering if I'll ever get to have her in my arms again.

Raya pulls away, but I sense her reluctance as her arms fall to her side. She gestures to the empty chair across from her, and we both sit down. "I'm so glad we could do this. Since everything that has happened, I needed to see you and make sure you're okay."

A young waitress stops by to take our food and drink order, halting the conversation. Raya orders a chicken and cheese quesadilla, and I go for the chicken burrito. After a long day at work, I need it.

When the waitress steps away after confirming our order, I return my attention to my best friend. "You look great, by the way. Did you get your hair cut recently?"

Raya smiles and flips her hair over her shoulder. "I did, actually. You're always so observant."

"Or it could be because I haven't seen you in forever." Even I hear the unspoken words hanging in the air. *I haven't seen you because I was held captive for a week.* I cringe internally and shift on the seat. "Anyway…"

Raya leans across the table, her pink manicured fingers wrapping around my hand in a gentle embrace. She offers me a sad smile. "If you want to talk about what happened, you know you can confide in me. I'm sure the media has been hounding you for these details, so don't feel as though you have to tell me."

The same waitress stops by the table to drop off our watermelon margaritas. She must sense the shift in emotion between Raya and me because she places the drinks down and leaves with a quiet nod.

I exhale a long breath and weigh my options. Raya would understand if I chose not to talk about my kidnapping and put it down to me not wanting to relive what happened. But after the text I received from my kidnapper… I don't know, I'm more confused than anything else. Throw in the fact I had sex with him and have been unable to stop thinking about him, I've got myself a messed up head and a person who doesn't know what to do.

Maybe getting the details off my chest will be therapeutic in a way. Raya is a great listener and isn't one to cast judgment on anyone. Granted, this might be the expectation given the contents of the details. But as my best friend, she will give me the advice I'm seeking as to what I should do about the situation I'm in.

If I don't say anything now, I never will.

"Okay," I breathe and squeeze her hand. "Buckle up because you're in for one hell of a ride."

Raya releases my hand and leans back. Within seconds the margarita glass is in her hand, her lips wrapped around the straw. "I'm ready. Lay it on me, Pae."

So, I do.

I tell her *everything*.

My lungs ache the more I talk, and my head becomes a jumbled mess with my chaotic thoughts. Between each part of the story from the moment I was kidnapped in the alleyway to the moment I was rescued, I stop to take a bite from the burrito I ordered and sip on my margarita.

Raya's eyes stay glued to mine as I speak. She doesn't utter a single sound, which I'm thankful for. I needed this moment to brain dump all over her and get my feelings out on the table, laying them bare. If she had stopped me to ask questions, it would disrupt the flow.

By the time I explain the text message I received from my kidnapper, I'm breathless. My burrito is now forgotten on my plate, and I'm desperate for another margarita.

Raya's eyes are wide as she gazes at me from across from the small table. She blinks slowly. "Oh, woah. That certainly was… a lot."

I exhale a sharp breath and run my fingers through the ends of my hair. "Tell me about it. I'm fucked up, aren't I? For what I did…"

Raya's hand shoots across the table to grab mine. "You're not fucked up, Pae. What you went through... no one should have to endure." Her hand squeezes mine gently. "You're a strong woman. I've always said that."

"I cheated on my fiancé." I blink back the tears forming in the corner of my eyes as my stomach twists in a painful knot. "And now I can't stop thinking about the man who kidnapped me. What normal person does that?"

I've disclosed my suspicions of Liam's infidelity to Raya. She has reminded me that without proof, I can't be sure that is what's happening. If he truly is cheating on me, then I'm no better than him.

My stomach twists painfully with the admission.

"It has to be Stockholm Syndrome," Raya responds, her voice low so the people sitting around us don't overhear. "It would explain everything. You said this guy was giving you food and water, and even spending time in your room. It would make sense that you've developed some sort of attachment to him for keeping you alive."

I ponder her words. Stockholm Syndrome? I never thought that could actually happen. Because what person would form a connection with someone who kidnapped them and held them captive? It could explain everything I've been feeling since I was rescued, though. And why I had sex with him.

Being locked in that small room for seven days would drive anyone crazy, making them feel alone and scared. Maybe I did develop an attachment to him because I was lonely and craved human interaction. It has to be...

"Maybe you're right," I murmur, my throat dry.

"If that's the case, you need to stay away from this guy, Pae. No responding to his messages or allowing him to see you in person. If you're worried about him, tell Liam and go to the police, okay? He sounds dangerous, and I don't want to even think about the possibility of losing you again."

I swallow hard and squeeze her hand. Raya's concerns are valid. I don't want a repeat of what happened to me. If keeping my distance from the masked man will ensure my safety and hopefully break whatever bond I've created with him, then so be it.

"I'm not going anywhere, okay?" I smile, patting the back of her hand. "Anyway, I need another drink. My treat this time."

Raya chuckles and leans back in her chair. "I hope you don't have plans for the rest of the night because I want to get so drunk I can't see straight."

"You and me both, Ray."

* * *

"Phew, Pae. What has gotten into you tonight?" Liam sighs contently beside me, his arm thrown lazily over my stomach. "You jumped my bones the moment you got home."

I exhale a low breath, my eyes focused on the ceiling. He's right. After my night with Raya, drinking too many margaritas to count and the recent discussion of possibly having Stockholm Syndrome, I wanted to prove that what happened with the masked man was a once off because I was lonely. That my attraction to him was just physical and nothing more.

The moment I walked through the front door—well, more like stumbled—I found Liam on the couch watching TV. His shirt reeked of perfume like it does most nights, but I didn't care. My drunk brain only had one thing on its agenda, and that was to sleep with Liam to remind myself who my fiancé is and why I need to stop thinking about my kidnapper.

While the sex was decent and I feel closer to Liam, I can't help but feel… odd. And I don't know why. I can't explain it. It's almost as if my mind is present but my body is vacant. Like I'm mentally here in the moment, but I'm physically somewhere else.

Yeah, back in the dingy bedroom with the masked man's hands roaming all over your—

"I'm going to get some air," I murmur, unable to meet Liam's eyes.

He hums in acknowledgment and rolls over to his side–away from me. "Okay, babe. Don't be too long."

I get out of bed, wrap my silk robe around my naked body, and scoop my phone off the bedside table. My legs move on autopilot, stepping out onto the small balcony that overlooks the front yard. A slight breeze nips at my skin, but I welcome it.

My elbows rest against the railing and I close my eyes, focusing on my breathing. The night is calm, which helps to quiet the chaos running rampant in my mind. If I could stay out here all night, getting lost in the breeze, I would. But I would eventually freeze given the time of year.

The dinging of my phone in my hand spikes my heart rate, erasing all the hard work I had just done. It's well after midnight, so who could possibly be texting me? Maybe it's Raya.

My phone bursts to life when I unlock it, the screen almost blinding. When I see UNKNOWN on the screen, the device nearly slips from my hand. My eyes snap up to sweep across the front yard, focusing on every nook and cranny of the tree line I can see.

Surely, he can't be here again.

DING!

Oh, shit.

Raya told me not to engage with him because it won't do me any good. I need to stay away from him because he's dangerous. Opening his messages will only continue to drag me into whatever game he's trying to play.

I should delete the messages and possibly get a new phone number.

I should walk inside, close the door, and go back to be with my fiancé.

I should not give *him* any more of my time than he's already taken from me.

But I don't do any of those.

No. Instead, I open the two messages, unable to stop myself.

Maybe I really am fucked up.

UNKNOWN: You make such pretty sounds, little bird.

UNKNOWN: But they sound prettier when they're for me.

My heart leaps into my throat. Is he watching me? How the hell does he know I had sex with Liam just now? Did he break into my house and watch from the shadows?

With shaky hands, I type a response. I keep my eyes focused on the phone, not wanting to gaze at the front yard for fear I would see him watching me from afar, his ocean eyes drawing me in.

PAE: Who are you and what do you want from me? I've seen your face, you know. I could report you to the police.

Maybe It's not ideal to threaten him, but if it'll get him to leave me alone, then so be it.

DING!

UNKNOWN: And yet, you haven't. Why is that? Is it because you don't want anyone to know what happened between us? Especially not your fiancé.

I close my eyes and focus on my breathing. This can't be happening. I need to shut this down before it gets out of hand. Maybe it's the alcohol coursing through my veins that is encouraging me to make bad decisions, but either way, I can't play into what this guy wants. Whatever that is.

PAE: You need to leave me alone.

I muster up whatever courage I have to turn and walk inside when another ding sounds from my phone, halting me in my tracks.

I should ignore him and change my number, but curiosity gets the best of me.

UNKNOWN: You can run from me all you like, little bird, but I will always catch you.

As I shove my phone into the pocket of my robe, I swear I feel the masked man's intense gaze on the back of my head from somewhere in the distance. Knowing he's been watching me spikes my heart rate and floods my veins with fear. And somewhere deep inside, a hint of desire I don't want to acknowledge.

What does he want from me?

CHAPTER FOURTEEN

Ace

Listening to bones splinter beneath my fist is like music to my fucking ears.

Drops of blood glide down my cheek, landing on my bare arm as it hurdles toward the man's fucked up face. The blow is sickening to my ears, followed by a deep groan. Again, hearing someone in pain because of *me* is something I could listen to all damn day.

"Please… stop." His breaths are labored, the syllables cracking slightly. His shaved head is slick with blood and sweat. "It wasn't… my fault."

I exhale a sharp breath and stand back, admiring my handiwork. The skin around his eyes is swollen to the point I'm sure I look like a blurry blob, and bruises are starting to form on his cheekbones which I'm sure are shattered inside his skull. Blood, both dry and fresh, litters his face.

He looks like fucking shit.

When I dragged his ass in here last night, kicking and screaming like a goddamn child, I knew he wasn't going to make it easy for me.

The poor bastard pushed my buttons, trying to talk me out of what I needed to do and attempting to escape, I knew I had to do something to keep him in place.

And that meant holding him against the large wooden boards lining the small room for occasions like this, and hammering two large nails through the palms of his hands. It made his screams louder, begging for help or death. No one came to his aid because not only is the room soundproof, but I was ordered to torture this fucker.

We've been going at this for hours. My knuckles are beginning to ache, but I welcome the pain. I fucking crave it.

It's a distraction from *her*. Silver hair. Eyes as green as the Amazon rainforest. A fucking sweet voice that damn well nearly brings me to my knees every time it echoes through my mind.

Fucking hell.

"Then whose fault was it, David?" My eyes meet his swollen eyelids. "Because, last time I checked, you were the one who fucked up the supply drop."

"I was jumped," he spits, frustration dripping from his words. "I had no idea those assholes were going to be there. I didn't… know they would take everything and leave me for dead."

"If I were you, I would have made sure you died before showing your face back here." I roll my neck from side to side, relieving the built-up tension. Despite the pain in my knuckles, I flex them, ready to continue. "Enzo is fucking pissed, and rightfully so. But luckily for you, he doesn't want me to kill you. Not yet."

David's lip quivers as he stares at me, his head falling forward. "Y-you don't have to do this, man. It wo-won't happen again, I promise."

"You're right, it won't happen again." Without so much as breaking eye contact, I reel my right fist back and land it square against his jaw. Blood spurts from his busted lips, spraying across the wall beside him. I grin at the sight. "Once I'm done with you, you're going to wish you were dead."

* * *

I STEP OUT OF THE ROOM, WIPING MY KNUCKLES WITH THE EDGE OF MY shirt. Maybe it wasn't the best idea to wear a white T-shirt given the bloody mess I left behind.

Two guards rush into the room, and moments later, David's limp and unconscious body is being dragged away. They disappear down the hallway, leaving me alone with my thoughts. Which isn't a good thing because they always drift back to *her*.

Every. Goddamn. Time.

Approaching footsteps from the opposite end of the hallway have my back straightening. I turn just in time to see Enzo, dressed in a pressed three-piece black suit with his dirty blond hair slicked back, flanked by two beefy guards. His black eyes find mine before traveling down to the blood-soaked shirt hanging from my frame.

An evil grin splits his face. "I see you had a good time."

"He may have squealed like a pig, but goddamn, was he fun to torture."

Enzo's aged features tighten as he clenches his jaw, his arms clasped firmly behind his back. "Did you get any new information from him?"

I run my hand through my messy hair, dried blood clumping some of the strands together. "He's adamant he knew nothing about those Bonanno fuckers jumping him. They came out of nowhere while he was down at the docks ready to make the drop."

Enzo exhales a long breath. "No one knew about the drop besides me and David. Which means we have a fucking mole."

Having a mole in the Gambino gang is unheard of. Enzo runs a tight fucking ship around here, keeping every member in line with a simple hard glance. No one would dare fuck with the Don, especially if you want to continue breathing through your mouth and not a straw.

Who would be game enough to tip off our rival gang about a drop? Someone with a death wish, I'm sure.

"If there is someone game enough to do that, I will fucking find them."

The corner of Enzo's mouth turns up in a smirk. "I know you will." He clears his throat. "Any news on the girl you kidnapped?"

I swallow hard and run my tongue over the inside of my cheek. "She's taken care of."

Enzo regards me for a moment, his intense blue eyes meeting mine. I don't need to say the words out loud for him to understand the meaning of those four simple words.

"Good," he finally comments. "And thank you for taking care of David."

"It's what I do." I shrug and shove my hands deep into the pockets of my black jeans. "Is there anything else you need from me?"

Enzo waves me off with a flick of his hand. "You've done enough. I'll see you tomorrow."

I bid my boss farewell and leave the mansion. Enzo likes to conduct his gang from the comfort of his lavish home. The hallways are filled with members, maids, and cooks. No matter where I walk, I encounter someone on Enzo's payroll. It's not uncommon for me to run into cops from the NYPD either. Most of the department is dirty, but it's none of my business.

Enzo hired me for one thing, and one thing only: to kill. If someone needs to be taken out or tortured for any wrongdoings, I'm the man Enzo calls. It's an easy job, really. And one I fucking love. Getting my hands dirty and my clothes messy is what I like to call a good day in the office.

The sky is pitch black when I step through the front door and descend the porch steps. My black Aston Martin DBS sits idle in the driveway. It's a reliable car and comfortable as hell. It was the first big purchase I made once the money started rolling in. And I have zero regrets about it.

Smooth leather meets the back of my jeans as I slide into the front seat. Cool air nips at my arms, but I welcome it. Even though it's winter, I find myself hotter than usual, my skin overly feverish.

I wonder if it has anything to do with a certain woman with silver-blonde hair and green eyes filled with innocence and kindness that bring me to my fucking knees every time I think about her.

My fingers flex around the leather steering wheel, my eyes boring straight ahead at the tree line surrounding the Gambino mansion. I know I should go home, but every fucking ounce of my soul demands I go see my little bird. Even if just for ten minutes.

I've been doing that a lot since the day she was rescued. I wasn't supposed to seek her out at the hospital, posing as a nurse and watching from close by as her fiancé sat by her side, holding her hand. It took everything in me not to march into the room and remind her that she didn't cry out his name when she came on my cock. But I didn't. I couldn't.

And maybe I shouldn't have followed her to her fiancé's parents' house and texted her from the comfort of the tree line. Seeing her squirm knowing I had found her and was watching from afar was enough to make me lose my goddamn mind.

I think the moment I realized I had grown obsessed with my little bird was two nights ago when I broke into her house and watched her have sex with her fiancé through the crack in their bedroom door. At that moment, with my fists clenched at my jaw and my teeth grating against each other, I knew I was a fucking goner for this woman.

I couldn't look away. Jealousy coursed through my veins like a disease, and it took every ounce of self-control to stay rooted in place. I hated seeing my little bird like that, but what did fill me with immense joy was the fact she wasn't enjoying it.

I could tell by the way her eyes flicked to the balcony doors as she rode his cock, as if she were looking for someone. That someone being me. Her moans sounded forced, and she seemed uninterested in the man lying beneath her.

As I walked out of the house that night and watched her from the tree line, waiting for her to come out on the balcony, I knew I couldn't stay away. For now, I was content with letting her know I was watching, enjoying the way she squirmed while reading each text message I sent. At least, until I decided my next move.

Because I know for a damn fact I'm not letting my little bird go.

Like most nights, I find myself standing in the tree line surrounding her property. From my position, I see her eating dinner with her fiancé. He's talking at her while she sits and listens. Although, I don't know how much she's truly listening because her gaze continues to sweep across the large floor to ceiling windows overlooking the backyard.

For a moment, I wonder if she spots me hidden in the darkness, watching.

She turns her gaze back to her plain fiancé and pushes food around her plate.

I grin, and reach for my phone lying in my pocket. If my little bird is looking for me, then I'm going to give her what she wants.

ACE: You waiting for me, little bird?

Paetyn's phone vibrates on the table beside her, and she rushes to snatch it up. Her fiancé is still yapping away, not noticing her attention is elsewhere. Her eyes flick across the message before winding. She glances out the windows briefly before typing back a response.

PAE: I told you to leave me alone.

I grin. Oh, this is going to be fucking fun.

ACE: Are you thinking about me while your fiancé talks? Do you wish it was my voice instead?

Her eyes flick between the device resting firmly in her lap and that bastard, who is still fucking talking.

I couldn't imagine living with that dickhead. He screams boring.

PAE: I'm not doing this with you, psycho. Leave me alone.

My tongue rolls in my cheek as I read her message. She's testing me, I know. Although her words say one thing, her body shifting in the seat as she awaits a response tells me she fucking loves this push and pull. She wants me but refuses to admit it to herself.

ACE: Psycho, hmm? I'm psycho enough to walk in right now, tie your fucking fiancé up, and make him watch while I fuck you. He'll hear you cry out my name and not his. Is that what you want?

PAE: You wouldn't dare....

ACE: Call me a psycho again, and see what happens, little bird. I'm a man of my word.

I watch as she squirms while reading my text. My cock is painfully hard at seeing her body react this way, and it takes everything in me not to touch myself at the sight of her.

Before she can type a response, the senator says something, snatching her attention away from me. She lowers her phone in her lap and resumes their conversation, forgetting about me.

I grit my teeth and slip my phone back into the pocket of my jeans.

One day, she will be mine. I'll make fucking sure of it.

CHAPTER FIFTEEN

Paetyn

I KNOW HE'S WATCHING ME.

Every day for the past two weeks, I've felt his intense gaze no matter where I am. The gym, leaving work, visiting Liam's parents, whenever I'm at the hospital visiting my mom, or even sitting in the living room with Liam by my side.

He texts me every day, too. Sometimes it's flirty messages or simple ones asking how my day was. I haven't replied since Liam caught me texting him during dinner after he threatened to burst into the house and fuck me in front of my fiancé. I could barely look Liam in the eye when he asked who I was texting. I had to play it off that it was Raya.

I couldn't deny the adrenaline rush coursing through me at the moment, wondering if my captor was crazed enough to make good on his threat. I mean, he kidnapped me, so I'm sure breaking and entering is nothing to him.

Either way, I couldn't bring myself to respond to any of his text messages. The more I engage with him, as Raya said, the more danger

I'm putting myself in. I thought it would be easy to ignore him, but it's a little hard when I feel his intense blue eyes on me or my heart skips a beat whenever he texts me.

What the hell is wrong with me? This Stockholm Syndrome shit is working overtime right now.

What I want to know is why he hasn't approached me. He follows every move I make, yet he hasn't shown his face.

Why?

What is he planning?

Whatever he's doing has me on edge. I'm constantly looking over my shoulder, wondering if he's going to be standing there, watching me with his intense gaze. Or will he pop out from the shadows of the trees around my house and break in to tell Liam what happened while he had me held captive? This man is capable of anything.

Not knowing his next move has consumed my mind for weeks. I think Liam is starting to notice something is going on because he has asked multiple times if I need to speak to someone about what happened to me. Each time I tell him I'm fine, but I think we both know I'm not.

He thinks I'm distressed and anxious about my kidnapping, but little does he know I'm on edge because I can't stop thinking about my captor.

Who is he? And what does he want from me?

All the unanswered questions I have swirling in my mind are slowly but surely driving me crazy.

With a huff, I step out onto the street after a long day at work. I'm finally caught up on all the appointments I missed with clients and am now back on my regular schedule, but I haven't been sleeping well. Which is understandable given my kidnapper is now stalking me. I can feel the bags under my eyes, and I know they're more than visible to those around me. But there is nothing I can do about it.

I wrap my coat tighter around my waist and merge with the rush of New Yorkers ready to get home. Liam has finally agreed to let me drive myself to work again, so I'm back to parking in the same lot I normally do, much to his concern, given what happened last time. I managed to ease his mind by reassuring him that if I ever feel unsafe, I will stop driving myself and go back to having a driver.

What Liam doesn't know is I have felt my stalker's presence behind me for the past seven days I've walked to my car. Every time I've entered the same alleyway he kidnapped me from, I expect him to come from behind and snatch me away again. But each time he doesn't, I get the sense kidnapping me isn't part of his agenda anymore.

So, what is? What does he get out of stalking me? If it's not to kidnap me, then what?

I don't understand.

A puff of air swirls around my head as I turn left, beginning the long, tortuous walk down the alleyway. I hold my breath, waiting to feel his presence like I have the past week.

And just like clockwork, I feel him. His eyes burn holes in the back of my head, sending a chill racing down my spine.

I don't tend to look behind me when I know he's there because I don't want to be part of whatever game he's playing. But today, a buzz hums in my veins, desperate for answers. It's killing me that I have no idea who this man is, what his name is, or why he's stalking me. The string holding my sanity and rational thoughts together is a thin thread.

If I don't say something now, this could go on forever. And I don't want that. I don't want to be his prey every night. I don't want to sit around and wait for him to make the first move.

I'm tired of this goddamn game.

At that moment, the string snaps in half.

With a huff, I whirl around with so much power a rush of air whips around me. He stops walking, his hands shoved deep into his pockets. Even in the darkness of the concealed alleyway, the blue in his irises is stark, sending an icy chill down my spine.

For once, he has a jacket over his shoulders, unlike every other time I've seen him in nothing but a T-shirt and jeans. The shadows lining the alleyway make it hard to get a good look at his features, but

I can make out the shape of his mouth and see his blue eyes glowing as they stare back at me.

If I didn't know any better, I would assume he was a stranger who happened to be going the same direction as me to get to his car. But I know better. Behind his casual outfit and unassuming stance, I know the intensity lurking in the depths of his eyes. A darkness licks at his sides that should have me running as fast as I can in the opposite direction. He's a monster hiding in plain sight.

But I don't run. Not in the opposite direction, at least.

Like a crazy person with a death wish, I clutch my handbag against my side and march toward him, my jaw ticking with determination and the need to get some goddamn answers.

His eyes hold my gaze as he watches me stalk toward him. He makes no move to leave or hide the fact that I caught him watching me. If anything, I see the corner of his mouth turn up in a smirk that has my vision blurring red at the corners.

Who the hell does this guy think he is?

"You," I start, barely containing the rage simmering beneath my skin. "Who the hell are you, and why are you following me?"

I stop in front of him, adrenaline igniting the blood in my veins as if I am high on drugs, and crane my neck back slightly to look him in the eye. The amused smirk he wears doesn't waver as he glances down at me, his large mass as still as a statue. I'm by no means trying to intimidate him, which would be impossible given his size, but I'm not leaving until I learn why he's doing this.

A deep chuckle rumbles in his chest. "Was that supposed to scare me?"

I frown, my teeth gritting together painfully. The fucking audacity of this guy. "If you don't tell me your name, I will scream."

The smirk touching his lips deepens. "Don't tempt me, little bird. Hearing you scream is like music to my ears. It would be better if it were my name tumbling from that pretty mouth of yours."

"That's a little difficult when I don't fucking know what it is."

Frustration gnaws at my side. Not only because of his stubborn ass making it difficult to get any sliver of information out of him, but because his words have gone straight to my core like a raging fire.

What the fuck is wrong with me? This man kidnapped me and held me captive. I should be afraid of him, not turned on.

"Ace."

"Ace?" I repeat, my heart thumping harshly at the base of my throat. "That's your name?"

He nods, his tongue darting out to glide over his bottom lip. "Happy now, little bird?"

I fold my arms over my chest, holding his gaze. "It still doesn't answer my question of why you're following me."

"Do you really want to know?"

"Yes," I reply, my frustration growing. It's like pulling teeth with this guy. "Why have you been stalking me since I was rescued?"

Ace steps forward, his body now inches away from mine. Light streams out from one of the windows in the building beside us, casting his features in a soft glow, nearly knocking the air from my lungs.

I haven't seen his face since the day I ripped off his mask, desperate to see the man behind my kidnapping. Back then, I couldn't deny how devastatingly handsome he was. But now, standing toe to toe with him in the darkness of the alleyway, those same feelings of attraction I felt at that moment come rushing back to me like a tidal wave.

My heart slams into my ribcage as he tilts his head to the side, his gaze roaming over the details of my face. "Because I want to, little bird. Ever since the night I took you to that cabin, I haven't been the same. I tried to tell myself it was nothing, that I would lose interest and move on, but the more I spent time with you, the more I realized I couldn't stay away from you even if I tried."

My eyes widen. "Wh-what?"

Ace straightens his spine. "Your innocent eyes drove me fucking crazy. To the point they were all I could see when I closed my eyes. It made me wonder if your body was as innocent, but when you were all but begging me to fuck you with those same eyes, I realized you were anything but innocent."

"I didn't beg you to fuck me," I spit, my blood boiling.

Even as I speak the words, my underwear is damp with desire. It's fucked up how turned on I am by his words, but I will never admit that to him. I don't want to feed into his already inflated ego. If anything, I would rather tell him I hated every second I spent with him, but we both know I'd be lying.

Instead, my plan is to ride the denial train until the cows come home.

Ace raises a brow at me. "I would beg to differ. I know what I saw. Your tight little body begged to have me touch it and to fill you with my cock. It's insulting that you would try to deny it."

Before I can even open my mouth to respond, I'm forced back against the wall to my right. A gasp explodes from my throat when something thick presses against it. I claw at it as I try to force air into my lungs, but it's no use.

My eyes clash with the depths of the ocean as they stare back at me. Ace's warm breath fans across my lips, his face inches from mine. My head is fuzzy from the lack of air but also the woodsy cologne I now associate with him.

Being in his position with his body pressed against mine and his forearm digging into my throat is far too much for me to handle. The fire in my core ignites in a ball of flames, and my lungs burn for air.

If someone were to turn the corner and make their way down the alleyway, they would be in for a shock when they stumble upon us. But even as people rush by the entrance to the alleyway, no one can see us hidden away in the shadows, out of sight. The thought deflates the tension in my shoulders.

The ache in my core is now a throbbing sensation, reminding me of how messed up I am for being turned on by this man pinning me against the wall and restricting my airway. I hate myself for the way I react to him, but I also can't deny the sense of thrill he gives me.

"Tell me, little bird. Does your fiancé know you fantasize about me when you're with him?"

My heart slams into my throat. "I-I don't know what you're talking about."

Ace grins, the sight menacing. "Oh, I think you do." The back of his fingers graze over the curve of my jaw, sending a tingling sensation across my entire body. "I've been watching you for a long time. Every conversation, every kiss, and every goddamn time you let him fuck you, I see it all. But I could see the vacant look in your eyes and sense your lack of interest in that loser."

He drops his forearm from my throat, allowing me one second to suck air into my lungs before his hand covers my mouth, pinning me against the wall again.

"I knew you were thinking about me, and how my touch lights your skin on fire. When you were bouncing on his cock, you wished it were me instead, didn't you?"

"You're sick," I manage to bite out. But what's sick is how fucking wet I am.

"I'll show you how sick I can be, little bird."

Just when I think he's going to let me go, his grip around my throat tightens, and our lips clash in a fiery inferno. The moment his lips graze mine, his tongue swiping over my bottom lip, demanding entrance into my mouth, I lose all self-respect. Why? Because I open my goddamn mouth like an obedient dog, relishing in the feel of his tongue sliding against mine.

Maybe I'm the sick one.

The kiss takes me by surprise. When we had sex, Ace never once kissed me or made a move to do so. He mentioned that he doesn't kiss and tell, so why has he all of a sudden changed his mind?

I come back to the same question I've been asking myself since the moment I woke up on that shitty bed in the room I was confined to: why me?

I'm defenseless as I submit to this man, my tongue eagerly tangling with his as he dominates my mouth. I clench my thighs together to ease the throbbing, but it's a useless effort. My arms hang by my side, unwilling to touch Ace. If I do, then I'm admitting defeat, and I'm far too stubborn to do that.

Ace sucks my bottom lip between his teeth before releasing it, his eyes finding mine in the darkness. A smug grin slips across his face, knowing damn well I enjoyed that kiss far more than I should've.

His free hand comes up to my face to rub a thumb over my swollen lips. "You can't hide from me any longer, little bird. Soon enough, you will be mine. And I'm a man who will stop at nothing to get what he wants."

He releases his grip on my throat, leaving me gasping for air. When I lift my head, Ace's back is to me with his hands shoved deep into the pockets of his jacket as he walks down the alleyway, joining the unsuspecting crowd of New Yorkers walking by.

With my heart hammering in my throat, I slide my back down the wall until I'm sitting on the ground, my knees pressed against my chest. My head drops into my hands, and I release a frustrated groan.

What the hell is happening? And why am I not scared of the man who kidnapped me?

CHAPTER SIXTEEN

Paetyn

It took me far too long to drag myself off the floor of the grimy alleyway and walk the rest of the way to my car. My body moved on autopilot as I drove home.

After the interaction with Ace, I was left feeling frustrated, both physically and sexually. I hated that I let myself feel affected by his words and even more so that I was turned on by them. It's wrong for me to feel this attracted to him, but it's almost as if my body has a mind of its own right now. No matter how many times I tell myself this is wrong, and I need to stay away from this dangerous man, I find myself thinking about him and the night we shared.

Ace is messing with my fucking head.

When I walk through the front door, Liam is pacing the living room with his phone pressed against his ear. His features are lit up with what I can only assume is joy as he speaks.

He doesn't see me walk in, so I take my leave and go upstairs to have a shower so as not to disturb him. Having a moment to myself before I face my fiancé after kissing another man is greatly needed to get my goddamn head screwed on straight.

By the time I make it to the bathroom and switch on the shower, I'm desperate to feel the hot water on my skin. Hopefully, it will wash away the shame of what occurred in the alleyway.

I close my eyes as I step under the spray of water, relishing in the feel of it sliding over my already inflamed skin that hasn't settled since leaving the alleyway. My hand rises to touch the base of my throat where Ace's large hand was wrapped around it. I'm hoping his grip wasn't tight enough to leave a mark. The last thing I need is to worry Liam more than he already is.

Ace's crude words slam into my mind like a raging bull. The thought of him watching my every move, including having sex with Liam, reignites the fire in my core. A dull ache throbs between my legs, making my head dizzy. Images of his fingers brushing over my jaw and the way his scent consumed my very being only add fuel to the already raging fire.

Fuck.

This is the exact opposite of washing away my shame. If anything, I'm creating more as I think about Ace.

My fingers glide over my swollen lips, remembering the feel of Ace's brushing against them with ease and determination, dominating my mouth like a starved man. Every lick and every suck went straight to my head, clouding my already tainted judgment.

"Shit," I murmur as I lift my hand to rest on the wall in front of me. "Get out of my goddamn head."

But even as I try to push any thoughts of Ace from my mind, I'm sucked right back in when I remember the way his ocean eyes watched me without shame and were filled with a passion I hadn't seen before. Everything about him is intense and invading, but it only fuels the attraction I feel for him.

Maybe I'm the starved man desperate for a bite of the forbidden apple.

Without thinking, my hand drops to my aching core. If I don't relieve the tension building, I fear I might burst apart at the seams. All because of the goddamn man who kidnapped me and is now stalking me.

I hang my head as my eyes flutter closed. My fingers brush over my clit. It's desperate to be touched. I drag my bottom lip between my teeth as I circle it. A shiver races down my spine at the contact, and it takes everything in me not to moan, but I manage to swallow down the sound.

My fingers set a steady rhythm, circling the swollen bud as I chase some goddamn relief. I rock my hips forward, needing a little more friction. As intruding as always, Ace's face flashes in my mind, eliciting a spark of electricity to spread beneath my skin.

"Shit," I murmur as I continue to touch myself, that same electricity a soft hum as it courses through my veins.

I slip a finger inside me, nearly losing my goddamn mind as stars dance across my vision. I'm unbelievably wet, which I hate as it has everything to do with Ace, despite how much I don't want to admit it. His filthy words and grip on my throat were all it took to get me to this point. And now I'm left to finish what he started.

A strangled gasp slips past my lips as I drag my finger back to my clit, my rhythm now relentless as I chase that high. Even as I barrel toward the orgasm waiting for me, I hear Ace's voice in my head.

That's it, little bird. Fuck your hand while you think of me.

And that's all it takes. I throw my head back, gasping as the orgasm rips through me like an unstoppable force. I'm barely able to hold myself up on the wall as my body vibrates with electricity and fire I've never felt on my own before. The feeling is intense and mind-numbing, making my toes curl with a wave of pleasure.

Fuck. What the hell was that?

I run my hand over my wet hair, unable to think straight. God, I'm a fucking mess. I can't believe I just got myself off thinking about Ace, the man who kidnapped and held me captive. While the orgasm gave me a moment of temporary relief, I'm even more on edge now than I was before.

"Pae?"

My eyes snap open at the sound of Liam's voice. Heavy footsteps enter the bathroom, and my spine straightens.

"Ye-yeah," I utter, my voice wavering slightly.

Guilt gnaws at my sides as I stare at the white shower curtain, knowing my fiancé is on the other side and has no idea of what I've just done.

"How was your day?" he asks, sounding awfully cheerful.

I clear my throat and grab my scented body wash, looking for some sort of distraction from my racing heart. "It was good. Busy day, as usual."

"And you got home without any problems?"

If you count being cornered by my kidnapper and being pinned against a wall by his strong hand around my throat as he kissed the air out of my lungs, then yes, I ran into a major fucking problem.

"No problems at all," I say instead as I lather body wash all over my body, hoping it'll clean away the shame clinging to my skin.

"Good," Liam says. "I'll wait for you in the bedroom while you finish up."

My heart thunders in my ears as I listen to his retreating footsteps. It isn't until the bathroom door closes that I release the breath I have been holding.

God, what am I going to do about the situation I have found myself in?

On the one hand, I care for Liam. I mean, he is my fiancé after all, and we share a lot of memories together. But do I actually love him? Or am I simply tricking myself into thinking that I do for the convenience of living this wonderful life we share together and his ability to help pay for my mother's medical bills?

But on the other hand, despite how fucked up it may be, I can't deny the physical attraction I feel for Ace whenever he's around. My body responds to his in a way that it never has for Liam or anyone before him. It's almost as if his touch, voice, and presence brings me to life, fueling me with a fire I have never felt before. It's addicting—and something I seem to crave when I'm alone and left with my thoughts about him.

I'm not in an ideal situation. I shouldn't be even making this comparison when Liam and Ace are nothing alike. Liam is a politician, but he is sweet and kind, and Ace is a criminal who kidnapped me and is now stalking my every move.

I can't believe this is happening to me. Surely, this has to be some fucked up dream.

But deep down, I know it's not.

What do I do?

With a sigh, I switch the water off and step out of the shower. I take my time drying my hair and wiping the beads of water off my body before wrapping the fluffy white towel around my torso and walking into the bedroom.

Liam sits on the edge of the bed, his royal blue tie loose around his neck. The sleeves of his white button up are rolled up to his elbows, making the muscles in his forearms bulge. His gray eyes meet mine over the lip of the crystal glass perched in his hand. He sucks down the amber liquid before standing, his eyes not straying from mine.

I do my best to smile like I'm not losing my mind over the internal battle raging through my thoughts. "When I got home earlier you were on the phone, so I didn't want to disturb you. But you seemed quite pleased with whoever you were speaking to."

"Oh, that." Liam tips his head back to drink the last of the whiskey before placing the glass on the bedside table. "That was my father. We were just chatting about how I'm now leading the polls by a landslide. If all goes well, and everything continues to work in my favor, I have a shot at winning the election in two months."

I walk toward the dresser and pull open the top drawer. "That's great to hear. I'm glad everything is working out."

Despite my lack of knowledge about politics and the fact I have little to no interest in it, I'm still happy for Liam. He's worked hard to get to where he is in his career, staying late at the office and working ungodly hours to put together his campaign, and putting in a hundred and ten percent into networking and ensuring he has the best team possible behind him so he can keep his seat. He works tirelessly for his constituents, from what he tells me. I don't know much about it, but I'm glad his hard work is paying off.

I gasp when I feel Liam's presence behind me. His fingers trail over the hem of the towel, teasing the skin on the back of my thighs as his breath fans my earlobe.

My heart rate spikes, but not because of anticipation or desire. No. If anything, it's guilt.

Liam slides his hand over the curve of my ass to my hip, resting it there. He presses his hard cock against my ass, wanting me to feel him. "I think we should celebrate, Pae. Don't you?"

I chuckle nervously, hoping he doesn't pick up on the tension in my shoulders and my erratic heartbeat. He presses his lips to my neck, kissing his way down to my collarbone as his other hand slides up to tease where the corner of the towel is tucked over itself, securing it in place.

Before he can pull the towel away, I stop his hand and turn to face him. Lust coats his gray eyes as he stares down at me.

"Maybe not tonight," I utter, my voice barely above a whisper. "I'm really tired and need to get dinner started. I'm sorry."

Disappointment passes over his features as his hands come up to rest on my hips. He steps forward so that his erection is now rubbing against my stomach. "Come on, babe. Seriously? I'm in a good mood because of the news I just got, and I want to share it with my fiancée."

I open my mouth to speak, but no words come out. What am I meant to say to that? *Sorry, I don't feel like having sex because I fucked my hand in the shower at the thought of another man.* Absolutely not.

I have every right to say no to Liam and leave it at that, but the happiness seeping into his features is only making the guilt chewing away at my stomach worse. I've betrayed him twice now with Ace, and it kills me that I've become a person who would do that. I can justify it all I like by telling myself that Liam is potentially cheating on me because of the women's perfume on his clothes, but I have no solid proof.

Maybe this might be the distraction I need to get my mind off Ace. At the end of the day, Liam is my fiancé, and that's not going to change. I'm going to marry him, whether Ace likes it or not. I also need to accept that fact.

Liam senses my hesitation, dragging his thumb over my bottom lip. "Fine, if you don't want to have sex, can you at least suck me off? I want to see these pretty lips wrapped around my cock."

I swallow hard and nod, fearing what my voice will sound like if I speak.

A grin splits across his face. "That's my girl."

With a flick of his wrist, Liam pops open the towel, and the material pools around my feet. As he undoes his belt and unzips his trousers, I lower myself to my knees, my heart thundering in my chest.

This is your fiancé, Pae. You need to forget about the monster stalking you and remember that this man is your life. Forget about Ace.

Liam shoves his pants down, freeing his hard cock. He slowly bumps the shaft as he guides it into my awaiting mouth. Now that I'm really looking at him, I can't help but compare his size to Ace. Where Ace is huge and protruding veins, Liam is smaller and less impressive.

Stop it, Pae. Focus on your fiancé.

A hiss falls from Liam's mouth when the head slips past my lips. "Fucking hell, Pae."

I clasp my hands together on my thighs as one of his hands slips into my wet hair, holding me firmly in place, while the other comes up to cup my jaw. Even though I was meant to be taking the lead on this, it seems Liam has his own agenda.

Liam rocks his hips forward, pushing himself to the back of my throat, groaning as he does. "I'm going to win the election," he grunts as he quickens his pace. "No one is going to beat me. I'm the best there is."

He continues to praise himself as he fucks my throat, but I zone out at his words. Instead, I focus on the night sky out the window and how the stars twinkle a little brighter out here than it does further in the city. I'm not one to get easily distracted in moments like these, but it seems Liam is only looking to get himself off, not caring about me, so I may as well not even be here.

As Liam mercilessly drives his cock to the back of my throat, I feel *his* eyes on me, lurking in the shadows. He may be hidden, but he makes his presence known.

My heart rate spikes, and my hands grow clammy. Liam may as well be invisible because all I'm focused on is *him*.

No matter where he is, I know he's watching. Waiting.

CHAPTER SEVENTEEN

Ace

For once, I'm not stalking my little bird.

This time, I have my eyes set on her loser fiancé. I knew politics was fucking boring, but it's even worse witnessing it with my own eyes. The mundane cream walls and white tiles in this building make me want to rip my eyeballs out of my skull.

It was easy to blend in with the crowd, posing as a janitor who cleans the hallways and offices. Given how far up each other's asses these people are, I knew I would be able to lurk the hallways undetected, keeping a watchful eye.

When I decided to watch Paetyn's fiancé today, just to see what he does throughout the day, I knew what I was walking into—boring people talking about an equally boring topic. I set up a video camera in his office when he left for lunch, hoping that when he returned he would give me something, anything, that would be of interest.

I have no idea what I'm expecting to get out of this. But I knew I had to find something incriminating to hold against this motherfucker with her. The sooner I get him away from my little bird, the better.

After I kissed Paetyn in the alleyway two nights ago, my obsession with her has only grown. I had no intention of giving her my lips because I'm not one to kiss on the mouth, the act far too intimate for me, but I couldn't help myself, not when she was looking at me with those innocent eyes. She is all I think about—her sweet voice on a constant loop in my mind, and her intoxicating scent simmering beneath my skin.

I'm consumed by every inch of her to the point it's maddening, but I welcome it. Crave it, even.

When I followed her home that night and watched through the open balcony curtains as that asshole fucked her mouth like it was his, all I saw was red. The deep-rooted obsession and desire to make this woman mine almost pushed me to the point of snapping his fucking neck just so he would stop touching her.

But I reined in my temper enough to not storm the room and show that fucker who Paetyn really wants.

She couldn't see me, but I know she felt my presence, and my eyes watching her from afar. I could tell by the way her cheeks flushed a light pink and her eyes stayed focused on the open space between us, as if she were wishing I would appear.

She wants me, even if she refuses to admit it.

From my position behind a cleaning cart I found in the storage room earlier, I watch the door to Liam's office. I managed to slip into the storage room undetected and stole a spare uniform lying on one of the shelves before taking the cart, using it as my shield from the eyes of the people walking the halls of the building.

No one is any the wiser as I lurk nearby, watching, waiting.

I check my watch and frown. Fifteen minutes. That's how long ago a leggy redhead waltzed into Liam's office and hasn't returned since.

I've been watching this fucker all day, and he has done nothing but attend meetings, talk with people in the hallway about boring political shit, and sit in his office doing God knows what. Besides this one little detail, he has been a very uninteresting fucking person to watch.

I glance over my shoulder at the near empty hallway. Most of the people in the building have long since left once 5:00 PM rolled around, with some lingering as they collect the last of their belongings. But not Liam Aster. When everyone in their respective offices left thirty minutes ago, he made no move to leave. Instead, he stayed put in his office, still joined by the unknown redhead.

My hands tighten around the handle attached to the cart. Whatever is happening in there, the video camera I strategically placed on the bookcase facing his desk will capture it. Whether anything of note is happening, I'm not sure.

I pretend to fiddle with items on the cart when the last of the lingering people in the hallway pass by, their eyes never straying toward me. Given I'm dressed in a janitor uniform and everyone else here is dressed in a suit, of course they don't take the time to glance in my direction. If anything, they view me as someone beneath them, no better than the dirt stuck to the bottom of their overpriced shoes.

If only they knew I was the devil in disguise.

After another long fifteen minutes, the hallway now empty, Liam and the redhead step out of his office. She adjusts her button-down shirt, her large tits barely contained by the material. Creases that weren't embedded into the fabric before she went in are now visible from where I stand at the end of the hallway. Her red lipstick is smeared ever so slightly, and a light sheen of sweat glistens over her pale skin. A noticeable glow that wasn't there before is now evident.

The redhead waves at Liam as she saunters down the hallway, fluffing her hair.

Liam bites his bottom lip as he watches her. He looks just as disheveled as the redhead. Not only is his hair a mess, but the forest green tie around his neck hangs loosely, and the top three buttons on his shirt are undone. But what makes me see red is the belt hanging loosely around his waist, and his unbuttoned trousers.

Oh, this motherfucker....

I fist my hands at my side, contemplating if I should shove him back into his office and allow him to get acquainted with my fists. The rage boiling beneath my skin is set to explode, but if it does, I'll be screwed. The last thing I need is for him to take notice of me and become suspicious. If he figures me out, this will have all been for nothing.

With my jaw clenched, I step back into the shadows of the hallway, my face growing hot with anger.

Liam taps the door frame before stepping back inside. I stand in silence for another ten minutes before he makes a move to leave for the night. When he shuts the door to his office, I'm surprised to see he doesn't lock it. Given he's a big shot politician, I would've thought he would lock up whatever shit he's hiding in there.

When he's out of sight, heading home to my little bird, I step out of the shadows and walk toward the closed door. It opens with ease, and I slip inside, making sure to shut it quietly behind me. The room is dark, save for the moonlight streaming in from the window behind the desk. I don't stop to gaze around the room, only focused on collecting the video camera from the bookshelf and getting the fuck out of here.

I snatch the device disguised as a book off the shelf and slip out of the room. I don't bother to put the cart away or take off the janitor uniform. I'm itching to get back to my car parked across the street and view the footage.

When I'm in the safety of my car, I plug the book camera into my laptop and wait for the footage to upload. My leg bounces beneath me, my patience wearing thin. If there is anything incriminating in this footage, I'll have to use some major restraint not to go to his house and kill the fucker. I already suspected he was cheating, but seeing it with my own eyes, and having evidence of such, will make me even more furious.

Touching what's mine is one thing, but thinking he can hurt her is another.

The uploaded file flashes on the screen. I waste no time clicking on it, watching as the video stream comes to life. The file is time stamped at nearly seven hours long, so I skip through the boring shit of him sitting in meetings, working on his computer and talking with whoever stopped by.

When I get to the last thirty minutes of the video, I stop, letting it play out. As soon as the redhead enters the room, closes the door behind her, and locks it, I lean back in the seat, my eyes focused on the scene playing out before me.

Liam stands from his desk and wastes no time pulling the redhead into his arms and kissing her. My fists clench on my thighs as I watch them make out, their hands all over each other. It gets worse when he bends her over his desk, flips her skirt up, and fucks her from behind.

That was all I needed to see.

I click out of the video and slam my laptop closed. Silence settles deep into my bones as I stare across the road at the building I spent all day watching this motherfucker. Fury gnaws at my sides. The fucking audacity of this guy.

What should I do with the information I've been armed with? It would be so fucking easy for me to leak this footage to the media and watch the assholes career and life crumble beneath his feet. I want to see him crash and burn for hurting what's mine.

Alternatively, I could use the video as leverage for him to leave Paetyn. I highly doubt a man of his status would want this type of scandal to reach the media, so if he were a smart man, he would leave what's mine and go about his life without so much as speaking a word about the footage.

Either option sounds appealing to me.

As I consider my options, captivating emerald eyes appear in my mind, followed by almost silver hair that looks fucking amazing wrapped around my fist. I grin as I remember the night we shared together out in the cabin. It killed me that she couldn't scream my name as she came undone on my cock. But she couldn't know who I was. It would ruin everything.

BUT NOW SHE KNOWS MY NAME, SO I'LL BE DAMNED IF I DON'T GET TO hear my name fall from her lips as I fill her.

My eyes flick to the closed laptop and the concealed video file hidden inside. Maybe I'll sit on what I should do with it for a little bit longer. Besides, I like this game I'm playing with my little bird. The one where she pretends she doesn't want me, but I know she's thinking about me, especially whenever she's with her fiancé.

If anything, it only fuels the obsession, knowing I have her at my fingertips but can't have her. At least, not yet. But soon.

I grin as I pull out my phone and click on her phone number. For now, I'll hold onto the footage until I need it. Who knows, maybe I'll find a need for it soon enough.

ACE: What are you wearing, little bird?

PAE: Go away.

ACE: You don't mean that, do you?

PAE: Yes, I do. Leave me alone.

ACE: Tsk. That's not what I saw in those pretty innocent eyes of yours two nights ago when your mouth was stuffed with another man's cock. You were looking for me, wishing you had your lips wrapped around me. You knew I was watching.

PAE: You're crazy and delusional.

ACE: Oh, little bird. Don't you know I like it when you talk dirty to me. Don't make me show you what I'm truly capable of.

PAE: I want you to stop messaging me and stalking me. I want you to leave me alone.

ACE: It's cute that you think I would just give up on you. I will stop at nothing to get what I want. That is you.

PAE: I'll never be yours, asshole.

ACE: We'll see about that, little bird.

CHAPTER EIGHTEEN

Paetyn

I'm not listening to a single word my client is speaking. The words are static in my ears as I stare at her, nodding when needed, but nothing she says registers in my mind.

It's not because I'm not interested in what she has to say. In fact, she's telling me about her inability to choose between two men in her life and how it's tearing her apart at the seams. This is certainly something I should be listening to as the person she has paid to help her and listen to what she has to say. But I just *can't*.

Her predicament makes me consider my own strangely similar one. I'm not in a position where I have to choose between two men, especially when there is only one right option in my case. But it doesn't stop me from thinking about Liam and Ace.

I shouldn't even have them together in the same thought when they couldn't be more different. Where Liam is kind and attentive, Ace is observant and dangerous. They are on different ends of the spectrum in terms of personality and even looks, and yet, they both occupy space in my mind.

Giving space to Ace in my mind which should only be occupied by my fiancé is unacceptable, and yet, I'm unable to get those damn ocean eyes out of my head, no matter how hard I try.

I clear my throat and force my attention on Mary as she continues to talk about how she can't decide whether she should continue seeing both of the men in secret or if she should pick one.

God, the irony of this isn't lost on me.

Once our session wraps up, I bid farewell to Mary with the promise of seeing her again in two weeks. After she leaves my office, I blow out a long breath and shake my head.

I can't get lost in my head, or even try to compare my situation to that of my clients. There shouldn't even be a situation to begin with.

After taking a minute to gather myself, I collect my handbag and step out of my office. Clarissa is sitting behind the receptionist's desk, her gaze trained on me as I approach her.

"What have I told you about sticking around past closing time," I scold, raising a brow at her.

She chuckles, not fazed by the warning in my voice. "Yeah, yeah, I know. I'm almost done, I promise."

I stop in front of her desk, gazing down at her. "Good. You work hard enough as it is. Do you have any plans for tonight?"

Clarissa nods. "Jayden is going to take me out to dinner and a movie. It'll be nice to get out of the house."

"Don't I know it," I murmur. "But have fun."

She drags her bottom lip between her teeth, her eyes flicking over my face. "How are you doing with everything? I mean… I'm sure it hasn't been easy these past few weeks."

I blow out a long breath. "I'm okay."

"Are you sure?" She raises a curious brow at me as if she doesn't quite believe the words coming from my mouth. "You seem a little… distracted. I get that the media has been a nightmare and you're probably on edge given what happened, so I wouldn't judge you if you said you weren't doing well. I'm here for you if you need to talk."

While her words bring me a sense of comfort, how could I possibly divulge the turmoil in my mind? If I don't understand what the hell is going on, how could I even begin to explain it to another person, much less my coworker?

"It's been hard to adjust to all the new changes in my life, but I'm okay, really." I offer a smile, but even I can tell it doesn't reach my eyes. "Anyway, have a good night, Clarissa."

"You too, Pae."

I wave goodbye and walk to the exit. As I step on the street and take the usual route to where my car is parked, it feels as though I'm on autopilot. I barely notice the people walking shoulder to shoulder beside me or the man on a bike who nearly hits someone behind me. The chill in the air does little to cool my inflamed skin.

The alleyway is dark, just like every other night. But for some reason, I don't feel *him*. His presence isn't suffocating me like it normally does, and his scent isn't lingering in the air. My brows crease into a frown as I spin on my heels, hoping to see him hidden in the shadows, but I'm left with nothing but disappointment when a street cat darts across the ground, seeking shelter in an empty crate beside a small dumpster.

Where is he? Not that I should care given he's a stalker who kidnapped me not that long ago. But for some reason, I feel… less safe without him around.

A heavy sigh falls from my lips as I turn to continue walking, only I'm stopped in my tracks at the sight of a figure approaching me, their hands shoved deeply into the pockets of their jacket.

My heart hammers in my chest. Any normal person would continue walking and maybe offer a smile to the stranger. Danger would not be high on their radar, especially if it's not something they've encountered before.

I, however, have alarm bells sounding in my ears at the sight of this person. Maybe it's their quick ended footsteps, hunched shoulders, or the way their head continues to gaze over their shoulder, as if they're checking no one else is around. Either way, this person screams dangerous to me, and I have nowhere to go.

The man is now a few feet away from me. I scream at my legs to turn and run, but they refuse to listen to my commands, betraying me. Flashes of the night I was kidnapped race through my mind, reminding me of how powerless I was in that moment. And the same thing is going to happen again.

Why are you so weak, Pae?

Now he's in front of me, the tip of a knife pressed against the base of my throat. I gag as stale cigarettes assault my senses, and he wraps his hand around the back of my neck, holding me in place.

"Give me all of your fucking money right now."

His voice is gravelly, and his breath is putrid. And despite the fear coursing through my veins, all I can do is stare at the man, blinking rapidly as I try to catch up to the gravity of the situation I'm in. *Again.*

"I-I don't—"

"Now!" he yells in my face, speckles of saliva landing on my cheek and chin.

My body vibrates as I stare at the man, his face half covered by darkness. I can still make out the light gray stubble on his cheeks and crooked yellow teeth. The windbreaker brushing against my arm has seen better days and the dark blue jeans he wears are covered in dirt and stains.

I scream at my body to put up a fight, to not let another man assume power over me. Being helpless is the last thing I want, but when my body shuts down, refusing to respond to my demands, there isn't much I can do.

I swallow hard, my throat dry. "Okay. Just… don't hurt me, please."

Before I can reach into my handbag, the man is wrenched backward, and the knife clatters to the ground. A rush of relief washes over me at the absence of the man trying to mug me, but it's soon replaced with confusion when I hear him grunting and pleading for his life, followed by a fury of skin meeting skin.

My eyes adjust to the scene before me, and my heart almost leaps out of my chest at the sight of the man gripping the mugger by the collar of his shirt.

Ace. He's here.

"Who the fuck are you?" Ace roars, his voice so deep it vibrates deep in my bones.

The mugger cowers beneath Ace where he cowers on the ground, his hands attempting to cover his face. "No-no one. I was—"

"If you don't get the fuck out of my sight in three seconds, you're going to wish you were dead instead of touching what's mine."

In the blink of an eye, the man scrambles to his feet and runs back the way he came, the knife forgotten about on the ground beside me.

I stare at Ace as he rises, his height intimidating as he stands in front of me. Despite his harsh exterior and the tattoos littering his right arm and knuckles, his eyes intense as they watch me, I know I'm safe with him.

"Are you okay?" Ace runs his knuckles over the curve of my cheek, the thick ring on his finger cold against my skin. "He didn't hurt you, did he?"

I shake my head. "I-I'm okay."

"Good," Ace says, his hand dropping to his side. "I'm sorry I'm late. I had something else I had to attend to first."

I blink at him. I want to ask what he was doing, but I'm not sure he would tell me if I did. Either way, I'm grateful he's here. If he hadn't stopped that guy… who knows what could've happened?

"I sh-should probably go." My voice is barely above a whisper, shock still lingering in my system.

"Wait." Ace wraps his hand around my wrist. His skin is warm against mine, and his touch gentle. "You shouldn't be going home alone, not if you were just attacked."

"But my fiancé…" I swallow hard, the words dying on my tongue. The thought of going home to Liam right now after he told me I shouldn't be driving myself to and from work is a recipe for him to tell me, *I told you so.* "He's probably wondering where I am."

"If he was worried about you, he would be here to ensure you get home safe. But do you want to know who is here, little bird? Me." His hand comes up to cup my cheek, our faces inches apart as he holds my gaze captive. "Come back to my place. I can keep you safe there."

My head is spinning from our close proximity, but also because he's right and I hate to admit it. If Liam was as concerned about my well-being as he claims he is, he would've put up more of a fight in having a driver take me to and from work, or he would be here himself. But he's not.

In the time I've been with Liam, I have never felt like I'm his number one priority. I'm below his career on that list, and while I'm proud of him for getting as far as he has, I can't deny that it does hurt that he doesn't put me first during the moments that matter. It makes me wonder if this will be the norm once we're married.

Although Ace makes a good point, I know I shouldn't go to his house with him. I don't trust myself when I'm around him or the way he makes me feel. Even now, I shouldn't be standing this close, soaking in his masculine cologne or the warmth of his skin.

But at the end of the day, I know I'm safe with this man. Call me crazy because I know I am, but I can't deny it. When he's around, even if he's lurking in the shadows or watching from afar, I know no harm will come to me. Even tonight, he came to my rescue when I needed someone the most.

That person should've been my future husband, but instead, it was my stalker.

I swallow hard and nod. "Okay. But only for a little while, and you have to promise to keep your hands to yourself."

Ace grins. "I can't make any promises, little bird."

God, I hope I don't regret this decision.

CHAPTER NINETEEN

Paetyn

PAETYN: Hey! I'm going to get dinner with Raya before I head home. There is left over food in the fridge if you want to heat that up. I'll see you later.

"Texting your fiancé, are you?"

My head snaps up at the sound of Ace's voice, and I slip my phone into my purse, not waiting for Liam's response. Ace has one hand on the steering wheel while the other rests on his lap. His eyes should be looking ahead, but instead they're on me.

Everything about him is intense, even when he's doing something as simple as driving a car.

I clear my throat and shift in the seat. "I don't want him to worry about where I am."

"And what did you tell him?"

"That I'm getting dinner with my friend."

Ace smirks and turns to look at the road, not saying a word. But he doesn't have to since I know exactly what he's thinking.

Thankfully, he doesn't comment on it. Instead, he surprises me by asking, "How was work?"

I blink at him. "Work?"

"Yeah."

I rub my hands together in my lap, staring at the side of his face as he watches the road. "It was… okay. Nothing to write home about."

"Do you like your job?" he asks.

"I do," I answer without hesitation. "I enjoy helping people. It's not the easiest job in the world, but if I can make a difference to at least one person's life, then that's enough for me."

Ace nods slowly, digesting my words. "Could you treat me?"

"Do you have something you want to talk about?" I throw at him with a raised brow. "You don't strike me as the type of person who would."

He hums, ocean eyes flicking to me. "And what type of person do you think I am, little bird?"

I swallow hard, eyes roaming over his sharp features, the curve of his jaw, and the inky strands falling around his face. Truthfully, I don't know what type of person Ace is because I don't know him well at all. At least, not what is on the inside. From the outside looking in, I can tell a lot about his character, but without the added depth of the details and experiences that shaped him, it's hard to get a read on him.

"From what I can see, you carry yourself with an air of confidence most men don't have. You have a stoic exterior, but seem to care deeply, and it's not something you try to hide. Everything you do is with precision and purpose. If I had to guess, you're the type of man who is ruthless to the bone, knows what he wants, and how to get it, and is fiercely loyal."

Ace rolls his tongue inside his cheek, eyes darting to mine when the car comes to a halt at a set of traffic lights. He regards me, the gaze long and intense as my words settle in the air around us. With how he's looking at me, I wish I could shove the words back in my mouth.

He chuckles and shakes his head. "You got all that from just looking at me?"

I shrug, my right leg bouncing with nervous energy. "I like to read people."

The light turns green, and the car jolts forward. "Well, I would have to say that is a fair assessment. Did you gather all of that when I had you at the cabin?"

"Mostly," I answer. "And partly from our encounters since."

He grins as he turns the car onto a quiet residential street. We turn into a driveway of a two-story house, the outside pristine with dark gray panels and a wooden porch attached to the front. The gardens around the house are well kept, and the lawn is freshly mowed. It looks like something out of a movie and not something I would have expected from a man like Ace.

He catches me blinking up at the house. "What?"

"Nothing," I murmur and clear my throat. "You have a nice house."

"It belonged to my parents before they passed away a few years back."

My head snaps to him, ready to ask about his parents since he brought up the topic, but he's already stepping out of the car, the door closing behind him.

I release a long breath before getting out and following him to the front door. The house is pitch black when we enter, but Ace flips a few switches, and the bottom floor is immediately illuminated with a yellow glow.

In this lighting, Ace is just as handsome as when he's lurking in the shadows of the alleyway, watching from a distance. Besides when he would bring me food in the cabin, I haven't seen him in anything but the natural lighting of the moon. Now, as I stand here gazing at him across the foyer, it's hard to deny just how attractive this man is.

"You have to stop looking at me like that, little bird." Ace's deep voice shocks me from my thoughts.

He's standing in front of me, his eyes gazing down at me with such intensity I shiver. His hand comes up to cup my cheek, the gesture stealing the breath from my lungs.

"Although, did you really think I was going to keep my hands to myself?"

My heart hammers in my chest, and in the silence of the house, I know he can hear it. I open my mouth to speak, but nothing comes out besides a puff of air. In the back of my mind, I thought he would keep from tempting me, but I knew deep in my heart he wouldn't. But if I'm being honest, I think my subconscious knew that would be the case and forced me to agree to go with him. I set myself up.

Ace's hand moves from my cheek to slip a strand of silver-white hair behind my ear. Warmth floods my skin where his fingertips graze. No matter how soft the touch or subtle the gesture, my body immediately reacts to him.

He lowers his head, our lips barely brushing as he holds my gaze. "Say the word, little bird, and I'll fucking devour you."

No. I should say no and push him away. It would be the right thing to do considering the circumstances and the fact I have a fiancé at home.

But the words refuse to leave my mouth, choosing to stay hidden in the back of my throat.

He grins at my lack of words and tilts his head to the side. "Or would you prefer I take what I want?"

The thought of him taking what he wants from me, with his dominating presence and intensity, should have me running for the hills. Instead, heat pools in my core, and I have to squeeze my thighs together to fight the dull ache beginning to throb.

When I don't respond, Ace's eyes darken, and his hands find my hips in a punishing grip. "Don't say I didn't try to play nice, little bird."

In the blink of an eye, a pressure presents itself against my stomach and my hair flies around my head as my eyes lock with the ground beneath me. I'm too startled to make a sound as Ace walks to the staircase behind us and takes two steps at a time with me over his shoulder.

All I can do is stare at the ground, stunned by what happened. He picked me up and flung me over his shoulder without so much as making a sound or breaking a sweat. If Liam were to do something like that, I'm sure he would struggle to get me over his shoulder considering his narrow shoulders and lack of strength. But Ace did it with ease, and I can't stop the blush from spreading across my cheeks.

What the hell have I just gotten myself into?

Each step down the dark hallway echoes in my head. I feel like a lamb going to the slaughter, unable to stop my fate even if I wanted to. And I don't.

It's hard to rationalize the situation I'm in when Ace has his thick arm wrapped tightly around my thighs, his fingers grazing over my skin as he stalks closer to the door at the far end of the hallway. I know this is wrong and I should get the hell out of this house, but I'm unable to find the strength to leave. To walk away and never see this man again.

But the thought is somewhat depressing to me and I can't figure out why. Maybe it has something to do with the fact that Ace makes me feel alive and safe. My body responds to his touch with ease, like I was made for him. When I feel him watching from a distance, my skin alights with thousands of tiny fires as adrenaline pulses in my veins.

What I feel when I'm with Ace is not something I can explain. It doesn't even make sense to me. But I know I can't continue to fight whatever is happening. If anything, I need to allow myself to give into this man, only if to see what becomes of it.

Ace pushes the door open with ease, stepping into the dark room. My head feels heavy from being upside down and my vision blurs with the darkness surrounding me. Seconds later, a light is flicked on, casting the room in a soft yellow glow.

I'm hoisted over Ace's shoulder, my feet landing softly on the ground. Unsteady on my feet, I glance around the room as my eyes adjust to the room. It's a simple space that suits a man like Ace well. Everything is black. And I mean *everything*.

A black king-sized bed frame sits opposite from the door, draped in black sheets and pillows. Two black bedside tables rests on either side with a gold metal lamp on each one. To the left, a large black dresser leans against the wall beside the only window in the room. For a large room, I would expect to see more furniture than this.

What does surprise me though is the black wooden chest on the wall to my right, sitting on the floor beside the door to the attached bathroom. Although it matches the rest of the room in terms of color, the sight of it sends a shiver racing down my spine.

What is hiding in a chest like that?

As if sensing my curiosity, Ace rests a hand on the small of my back, his mouth inches from ear as he whispers, "Would you like to see what's inside, little bird?"

My heart rate spikes at the proximity of his chest to my back and the way his warm breath fans against the shell of my ear. I eye the chest, wondering what could possibly be inside.

Maybe it's loaded with a lot of weapons or something more sinister that I wouldn't be able to wrap my head around. Anything is possible with Ace, given how little I know about him.

When I don't respond, Ace chuckles. "Maybe you're not ready yet."

"I'm ready." The words tumble from my mouth before I can stop them. I swallow hard. "I mean, I want to see what's inside."

Ace steps out from behind me and walks toward the mystery chest. "Okay, little bird. If you say so."

My heart is in my throat as I wait for him to flick the latch open. The hinges groan as he lifts the top up, revealing the hidden contents inside. I step forward to get a better look, my hands fisted at my side to stop the trembling threatening to consume me.

As my gaze sweeps across the contents lying inside, the pounding of my heart intensifies. My eyes flick between Ace and the box, unable to believe what I'm seeing. "W-what is this?"

Ace drags his tongue across his bottom lip, his ocean eyes locked on me, studying my reaction. "A side to me only some are privy to know."

"And what side is that?"

"Maybe you'll find out."

I'm unable to tear my eyes away from the abundance of sex toys. It's unlike anything I've ever seen. Some of the items among the ropes, handcuffs and bondage restraints are foreign to me. Something I never thought I'd see, and yet, arousal pools between my thighs at the sight of them and my heart jackhammers against my rib cage with anticipation.

The thought of Ace sharing this side of him with other women brings a pang of jealousy. But I quickly push the emotion away because I have no right to feel that way about a man I hardly know.

Ace steps forward, invading my space with his cologne and intense gaze. I tip my head back to meet his gaze. "Is this the type of distraction you were looking for?"

Before I can think about it, I nod, my body trembling with desire and anticipation.

A slow, lazy grin slides across his handsome features. "Tell me, little bird. Does your fiancé know you have a darker side to you? Because I can see it reflected in your eyes."

I swallow hard. In the bedroom, Liam is a fairly vanilla person, and while I respect that he doesn't want to explore other kinks or switch things up in the bedroom, I can't deny that I have always wanted *more*. What that entailed exactly was unknown to me. At least, until now.

"No," I murmur, my voice barely above a whisper.

"Well, I can see it written across those pretty features of yours." Ace's hand comes up to rest on my cheek. "And I plan to show you what you've been missing out on."

He drops his head to capture my lips, rough and demanding. My arms instinctually lift to wrap around his neck, but his hands capture my wrists before I can touch him, forcing them at my side while his tongue plunges into my mouth, claiming the space.

Not being able to touch him forces a whine up my throat, and my veins thrum with anticipation. I want to touch him, to feel his warmth against me, but his tight grip on my wrists leave no space for wriggle room, so I'm left with no choice but to kiss him back.

His tongue swipes across my bottom lip before nibbling on the skin. My eyes roll to the back of my head as stars dance across my darkened vision. I had no idea a man could kiss like this and illicit such a fire deep in my core that I feel it spreading across every inch of my body.

Ace pulls away, a devilish smirk on his sharp features. "Strip for me."

My eyes nearly bulge out of my head. "W-what?"

He walks past me and sits on the edge of the mattress, settling his gaze on me. At no point does he give away what he's thinking. I hate that he is able to hide his thoughts so easily behind those stormy eyes. I just want to know what is going on inside that head of his.

I turn to face him. "You want me to strip?"

He nods.

"*Now?*"

"Now, little bird." Ace places his hands on the duvet behind him and leans back, eyes locked on me. "Or do you need a hand?"

My cheeks flame at his suggestion. The last thing I want is for him to help me undress when it's clear he wants a show. Although I'm fucking nervous in the presence of this man, I don't want him to see how much he affects me. Not yet, at least.

"Okay," I murmur and begin to unbutton my blouse. My fingers tremble over each button, and I just know I must look like a fool, but I soldier on.

By the time the fabric falls away, and I pop open the button on my trousers, the tips of my fingers tingle with warmth and my pulse thumps at the base of my throat. Ace's eyes on me are intense as they watch my every movement. Part of me wants to put an end to this for fear of embarrassing myself, but the other part is desperate to know what happens next. Especially with the chest of wonders behind me.

"Slowly," Ace groans as I slide the material of my pants down my thighs. He fists the sheets behind him in his hands as his gaze locks onto my lower half.

The fire in his eyes and pulsating of his jaw as he clenches ignites the burning of my core. Arousal pools between my thighs as I step out of my shoes and slide the pants off, going at a pace approved by Ace, judging by his obvious erection.

Oh, good lord.

What have I gotten myself into?

When I'm left standing in my black lace underwear and white blouse hanging from my shoulders, Ace stands and steps toward me, towering over my frame. My breath hitches in my throat when he slides the material off my shoulders.

"Kneel on the edge of the mattress with your back to me."

A chill races down my spine at his words. When I meet his gaze, the blue in his irises are darker than usual and laced with an emotion I can't read. I swallow hard at the sight of them.

Without saying a word, I step around him and kneel on the edge as he instructed. I rest my hands flat on my thighs and stare out the window opposite me as a way to distract myself from whatever Ace is doing behind me. I have no idea what to expect after seeing what he had hidden in the chest. But what I do know is my body is thrumming with nervous energy as I wait to find out.

A gasp slips past my lips when the hook of my bra snaps open, the material falling from my shoulders and onto my lap with ease.

"Put your hands behind your back," Ace commands gruffly, his voice low.

Swallowing hard, I do as I'm told. My core is throbbing and in desperate need of attention or some goddamn relief because this is too much.

A slightly rough material closes around both of my wrists, strapped down by what sounds like Velcro. I try to pull them apart, but whatever is secured around them doesn't allow much room for movement, forcing my shoulders back.

Ace's fingers brush over the base of my neck before a similar material is wrapped around it, secured by a Velcro strap. My heart hammers in my chest as I put two and two together.

Holy shit. He has me bound.

He traces the curve of my spine, a low hum sounding from his throat. "So fucking beautiful, little bird. Every inch of you is screaming for me to touch it, mark it, claim it. You were fucking made for me."

I gasp when his hand comes down on my right ass cheek, the sound echoing throughout the room. The stinging sensation quickly morphs into pleasure, and I bite back a moan.

Ace steps away and rummages through the chest, unaware of the fog swimming in my mind and the heat coursing through my veins.

"I'm going to go easy on you this time, little bird. But next time, I won't be able to say the same thing."

He appears behind me again, his chest brushing against my back and his erection pressing into my ass. My breath catches in my throat when his hand grazes over my hip, and up to my stomach. His fingers leave a trail of heat behind them, sizzling my skin.

I shiver under his touch.

"Your body reacts to my every touch," he muses, his fingers dancing over my skin where they stop at the curve of my breast. "Almost as if you were fucking made for me."

A sharp pain sparks from my nipple as something roughly pinches it. I gasp, my chest heaving as I look down to find the source of pain. My eyes widen at the metal clamp attached to a chain capturing my nipple between it. The pain of it squeezing me to the point I fear it's going to do more damage than good quickly morphs into a whirlwind of pleasure I have never experienced before.

Heat pools between my thighs as another one clamps down over the other nipple, both of them now attached by a chain.

Holy fuck. What the hell is happening right now?

Ace's warm breath fans over the curve of my shoulder as he reaches around me. "Head back."

I do as he says and tilt my head back, my breathing coming out in pants and my head swimming with a fucked up concoction of pleasure and pain. I don't know what Ace is doing, nor can I focus on his movements when all I can think about is the nipple clamps and how they're driving me wild.

Ace leans back and tugs on the chain attached to the clamps, and my head drops forward.

What the fuck...

"Are they..."

I don't get the chance to finish asking the question because I already know the answer. Not only are my hands bound behind my back with a collar wrapped tightly around my neck, but now the nipple clamps are also attached to the collar.

Imagining what I look like at this moment, on my knees and bound in front of the most attractive man I have ever laid eyes on, causes a flood of arousal to pool between my thighs, making a mess of my panties.

"You're so fucking beautiful, little bird," Ace murmurs behind me, his hand tracing the curve of my spine. "And you're all mine."

His hand glides over my ass and slips between my thighs. Heat spreads across my cheeks the moment his fingers make contact with my damp panties.

"You're fucking soaked," Ace says, his voice strained. His fingers swipe over the material, moving back and forth, teasing me.

I close my eyes as a moan slips past my lips. Not being able to move or touch him is driving me to insanity, and the pressure of the clamps on my nipples is not helping.

A strangled gasp sounds in the air when Ace pulls my panties to the side and slips two fingers inside of me. The pressure of him pressing against my walls has my vision blurring at the edges. Too much is happening right now and I'm unable to keep up.

Ace drops his mouth to my neck, his lips attaching to the skin as he sucks and bites, drawing another moan from me. He pumps his fingers into me, the rhythm slow at first before gaining momentum. I'm all but panting as he drives into me, taking what he wants.

He pulls back from my neck and presses a delicate kiss to the shell of my ear as he stops moving his hand. I whine at the sudden loss of movement.

"Bounce on my fingers, little bird. I want to see you fuck my hand like it's yours."

Needing to feel him moving inside me again, I rock my hips forward, chasing that friction. A deep groan sounds from Ace's throat as he stands unmoving behind me, his eyes burning holes in the back of my head.

With a shaky breath, I lift myself up ever so slightly before dropping back down, feeling his fingers sink inside me. My eyes roll back in my head as a wave of pleasure crashes over me.

"That's it," Ace coaxes, his voice strained. "Fuck my hand. I want to feel every last inch of you."

I don't know what came over me, maybe it was his filthy words or the nipple clamps going straight to my head, but I pick up the rhythm and slam down on his hand, desperate to feel more. Heat blooms in my core and I'm close to rushing over the edge.

Everything is beginning to feel like too much, namely the way I'm bound and fucking Ace's fingers, but also his intense presence behind me, urging me forward. My vision is non-existent and my breathing is ragged as I bounce up and down, waiting for the tidal wave of pleasure to hit me.

I just want to—

A hand on my shoulder stops my movements. Ace pulls his hand away, and I whine in frustration at the loss of contact.

He wraps his hand around the back of my neck and pushes me forward until my face is pressed firmly into the soft duvet with my ass in the air. The clamps tighten around my nipples in the new position and I cry out, wriggling under Ace's grip.

His hand slides over the curve of my ass as his fingers tighten around my neck. "Don't move a muscle, little bird. If you do, I'll have to punish you."

My skin tingles at his promise. I don't know what his definition of punishment is, but a voice in the back of my mind is demanding I find out.

Ace releases my neck and steps back, the sound of his belt clinking filling my ears.

I hold my breath as I shift on the bed, hoping to bring some relief to my poor nipples. But that earns me a harsh smack on the ass.

"Fuck," I groan as the stinging sensation intensifies.

"I told you not to move," Ace warns, his voice dangerously low. "I wasn't kidding when I said I'd punish you."

Heat rolls in my core and I exhale a shaky breath as I listen to him pull the belt through the loops. It falls to the carpeted floor with a soft thud, followed by the dragging of a zipper.

My heart hammers in my chest as I listen to Ace's movements. It's driving me crazy not being able to see what he's doing, the anticipation gnawing at my sides, given the current position I'm in.

"Ace," I murmur before I'm able to stop myself. "Please…"

"Please what, little bird?"

"Touch me, please."

A hum vibrates in his throat. "Is that right?"

I nod, unable to find my voice as I breathe heavily against the duvet.

"Have you been a good girl, Pae?"

I open my mouth to speak but only a puff of air escapes. My lack of response earns me another smack on the ass, harder than the previous one. I yelp and fist the bed sheets, riding out the sting sizzling beneath the raw skin.

"I asked you a question. Have you been a good girl?"

"Ye-yes," I stammer, breathless.

"Yes *what*?" Ace probes, his voice thick with lust.

"Yes, I've been a good girl."

My heart is jackhammering in my chest as the words leave my mouth. I stare at the door to my left, waiting for Ace to do something or say something, but all I'm met with is silence. My knee jerk reaction is to look over my shoulder to see what he's doing, but the threat of being punished rears its head, so I don't move a muscle.

After a long moment, Ace slides his hand over the curve of my ass and tears the edge of my drenched panties. "I need you to tell me you're mine."

My eyes snap open. "Wh-what?"

His hand slips beneath the material to drag over my slick folds, teasing me. "Tell me you're mine, Paetyn. I want to hear you say it."

"I-I—" *I can't do that*, I want to say, but the words die on my tongue. How could I possibly say something like that to a man I barely know? The same man who kidnapped me and held me captive for a week. The same man who has been stalking me ever since and could potentially be a dangerous man?

"No?" he murmurs and pulls away, adding to my growing frustration. "One day you'll tell me without my having to ask, little bird. Because believe it or not, you are mine."

My arms are tugged back at the same time I feel the crown of his cock nudge my entrance. The pressure of Ace slowly sliding into me and the cuffs around my wrists as my back is forced to arch has my vision blurring at the edges and a groan bursting from my lips.

"Fuck," Ace grunts as he bottoms out. "You're perfect, little bird, and so fucking tight."

All I can manage is a moan in response as he drags out of me only to slam his hips forward, driving deeper into me. A shock of pleasure zaps through my veins as my nipples brush against the duvet, the clamps somehow tightening around the raw skin as Ace picks up the pace.

He releases my bound hands to grip my waist as he drives into me, muttering curse words under his breath. With the position I'm in, bound with my ass in the air, a new wave of sensation flows through me like a tsunami, crashing into every crevice of my body. It's almost too much to handle, but somehow, I manage to stay focused and zero in on the filthy groans leaving Ace's mouth and the way he fills me.

He truly is unlike any man I've ever met. Being with him makes me feel alive and free to express my deepest, darkest desires. He has brought out parts of myself I didn't know existed until I met him, and now it's all I crave. Because of him, all I want is more. And I know he's the only person who can give me that.

"Ace," I cry, unable to handle the pressure building rapidly in my core. "I can't—"

"I don't fucking care if you're engaged to that loser," Ace grunts as he jerks his hips forward, meeting with relentless thrusts. "He doesn't make you feel the way I do. In fact, he doesn't deserve to fucking see you this way or hear the sweet sounds you make."

He brings a hand down on my exposed ass and it just about sends me over the edge. I'm breathless and my head is starting to spin, but I focus on Ace and his presence. I'm addicted to the feel of his fingers digging into my skin and the way his cologne wraps around me like a warm blanket.

"Shit," Ace hisses as he picks up the pace, the slapping of our skin almost deafening. "Fuck!"

I don't see the blinding light coming or notice the fall over the edge of the cliff, but I sure as fuck feel it in every corner of my body. My body trembles as I come, the orgasm shocking me to my core and stealing my vision as I ride the wave.

"Ace!" I cry, shaking violently as he continues to fuck me, chasing his own release.

Moments later, Ace pumps into me slowly, filling me with his release. Each drag of his cock through my sensitive walls has me trembling all over again as I come down from the high. My head is blank as I stare at the wall, trying to make sense of what the hell just happened.

Ace just blew your fucking mind is what happened.

"Fuck," Ace strangles out as he pulls out of me. His absence has me biting back a cry. "Jesus fuck, Pae."

He tugs on my bound hands, pulling me back until I'm on my knees. My body feels like jelly as he reaches around and takes the clamps off what I'm sure are bruised nipples. Cool air bites at the raw skin and I hiss at the sensation. Ace undoes the straps around my wrists, freeing my arms that are aching from the awkward position, and then removes the collar around my neck.

"You did so good," Ace praises. He presses a delicate kiss to my shoulder. "Maybe you can handle this side to me."

I think I'm in shock as I stand from the bed and turn to Ace. He's completely naked with a slight sheen of sweat coating his smooth skin. Every muscle in his chest, arms, and abdomen are taut from exertion. If I wasn't so dazed from the insane orgasm I just had, I would drop to my knees and repay the favor.

Ace tucks a strand of hair behind my ear. "Are you okay?"

I nod. "I'm okay."

"Let me get you cleaned up."

I silently watch Ace disappear into the attached bathroom, followed by the sound of rushing water. Moments later, he returns wearing a pair of sweatpants and holding a damp cloth. My heart pulses at the base of my throat as he drops to his knees and swipes the cloth between my thighs, collecting every last drop of our bodily fluids.

He did the same thing when we were back in the cabin. I hadn't expected him to perform any sort of after-care for me then, but I appreciated the effort. Now, seeing him on his knees as he works to clean me has my heart swelling with an emotion I'd rather not think about.

"Thank you," I murmur when he stands, his eyes locking with mine.

"For what? "

"For cleaning me," I admit, my cheeks warm. "And for… that."

A grin splits across his face. "You don't need to thank me. I would do anything for you."

I blink at him, letting his words settle around me before I look away. Wordlessly, I step to the side and scoop up my clothes, holding them close to my chest. "I should probably go home."

Liam is probably wondering when I'll return. Guilt settles low in my stomach knowing that I'm lying to him about my whereabouts, and while part of me feels terrible about it, another part of me knows I can't resist Ace and the way he makes me feel. A fucked up war is raging inside my head and I don't know which side is going to win.

What I do know is I can't stay here with Ace for a second longer, not when my emotions are on such high alert. Having his intense presence in proximity will only mess with my head more than he already has since the moment he walked into my life.

Well, forced his way in.

Ace stands behind me, his hand sliding up my arm to rest on my shoulder. His warm breath fans across the curve of my neck, sending a shiver racing down my spine. "Just so you know, I'm not going to stop until you're mine. Even if I have to pry you from that fucker's hands, I'll gladly do it. I would do anything for you, little bird, even if it means burning the fucking earth to the ground until I have you."

I swallow hard, my breathing shaky as I slip my hands through my blouse sleeves. "Please take me back to my car, Ace. I have to go home."

He steps away, taking with him the warmth I crave and the presence that keeps me safe. "As you wish, little bird."

* * *

THE TELEVISION IS ON WHEN I WALK THROUGH THE DOOR, MY SHOES hanging from the tips of my fingers. When I poke my head through the doorway to the living room, Liam is nowhere to be seen. It's not even 10:00 PM, so surely he's awake.

When I walk into the kitchen, I spot the back of Liam's head as he sits at the island, a glass of whiskey in his hand. My heart stills in my chest at the sight. Liam isn't one to drink hard liquor often, unless he's had a particularly long day at work.

"I'm home," I say as I walk further into the room. He doesn't flinch at my words but lifts the glass to take a sip as I round the island. "Did you make something for dinner?"

Liam lifts his eyes to meet mine, and I nearly stumble back at the intensity of them. The gray in his irises are like a raging storm cloud, ready to bring chaos when it makes landfall. His hair is pushed back from his face with his tie hanging loosely around his neck. I've never seen Liam like this before.

"Are you okay?" I ask, my voice barely above a whisper.

"Are you cheating on me, Paetyn?"

His words hit me like a semi-truck, tearing through my heart and lungs before shooting out of my back. I blink, trying to process his words.

He takes my silence as answer enough.

"I fucking knew it." He runs his hand through his hair and shakes his head. "I can smell men's cologne on you even from here."

The mention of cologne kicks me back into reality, and I frown. "Don't think I haven't noticed the women's perfume clinging to the collar of your shirt for months, Liam."

He stands and slams his hands down on the countertop, his eyes locked with mine. "Stop trying to change the subject. You're cheating on me."

"I'm changing the subject?" I ask, exasperated. "You're one to talk. You're accusing me of cheating on you because you can smell men's cologne? I work with male clients every day, so it could be because of that. You, on the other hand, come home smelling of women's perfume and often times have lipstick smudged on your collar. Don't think for a second that I'm some sort of idiot because I'm not, Liam."

His jaw ticks as he regards me, his gaze hard. "You don't know what you're talking about."

"Don't try to tell me I'm wrong because I know what I've seen. So before you start accusing me of something, maybe you should check yourself first."

He opens his mouth to say something, but instead, he grabs the glass beside him and launches it at the wall beside me. I gasp and cover my face. Tiny shards of glass nick at my arms, but not enough to seriously hurt me.

"I can't even look at you right now." He pushes away from the island. "I'm sleeping in the spare room tonight."

And with that, he storms away, leaving me to clean up the mess he created and pick my heart up off the floor. I stare after him, at a loss for words as to what just happened. The look in his eyes is unlike anything I've ever seen, and his anger was brutal. But what hurts the most is that he refuses to take accountability for his actions, claiming I'm the only one in the wrong.

I lower to my knees, scanning the pieces of glass surrounding me. I should take this as my sign to leave Liam because it's clear neither of us are happy, but I have my mother and her health to think about. If I leave now, she won't get the help she needs. But if I stay, I have to live with a man who doesn't care about me like I thought he did.

With a sigh, I scoop the shards into a pile, ignoring the sharp pain shooting up my arms as the glass slices into my fingers.

What the hell am I doing?

CHAPTER TWENTY

Ace

It's taking everything in me not to snap the motherfucker's neck. But I have to wait and be patient. Not only am I in public, watching as the rat lurks the street, his beady eyes following women as they pass by, but I can't give myself away.

Not yet.

I lean against the streetlamp beside me, my eyes locked on the man I now know as Johnnie Abrams. After my encounter with him three nights ago when he attempted to mug my little bird, I did some digging into him and used my connections to learn everything I could about him.

Nothing of importance turned up. He is nothing but a common street thug who is well-known to the police for his petty crimes, and yet, he still has the ability to stalk the streets, searching for his next victim. But not for much longer once I get my hands on him.

Johnnie leans against the wall of a building beside a dark alleyway, much like the one Paetyn walks every night after work. A cigarette hangs from his lips as he lights the end of it. With it being almost midnight, there aren't many people walking the streets, which is good for me.

From my spot in the shadows across the street, I watch as he exhales a puff of smoke and pulls out his phone. I've been watching him for hours since I followed Paetyn home after work, ensuring she got home safe. Although she knew I was there, she didn't try to speak to me or even look in my direction. It annoyed me because, after the night we shared together, I had expected there to be a shift between us, but it seems she still wants to play hard to get.

Lucky for her, I'm not one to give up easily on something I want.

This is the first time tonight Johnnie is alone and away from watchful eyes. If he isn't hanging around with his sleazy friends, laughing like hyenas, then he's always on the move, walking the streets as if he has no destination in mind.

But now, he's alone and distracted.

It's the perfect time to strike.

I push off the streetlamp and shove my hands deep into the pockets of my leather jacket. Sticking to the shadows, I make my way across and approach Johnnie. He's too distracted laughing at something on his phone and puffing on the cigarette between his teeth to see me coming–or the fist that collides with the side of his face.

A deep groan bubbles from within his throat as his hand flies up to cup his red cheek. His phone clatters to the ground, as does the cigarette. When his eyes meet mine, fear immediately consumes them, and his face falls.

"Y-you—"

"Yes, me. Your worst nightmare." I grab the front of his stained white T-shirt and land another punch to his swollen cheekbone, smiling when I feel the bone crack under the force. "I believe you fucked with the wrong woman last night, and you're going to learn what the consequences are for touching what's mine."

Blood drips from his face as his eyes widen. "No, no, no—"

With one last punch to the side of the head, Johnnie falls limp in my arms, out cold. I haul him over my shoulder and start the walk back to my car.

I'm going to find out why he attacked my little bird, and the method isn't going to be pretty, that's for sure. He will pay for trying to hurt her.

If Paetyn thinks I'm a psycho, then I may as well continue to play the part.

* * *

THERE IS NOTHING I LIKE MORE THAN THE PAINED SCREAM OF A MAN IN agony at my touch. In fact, I would go as far as to say it's my favorite sound, second to Paetyn's laughter in the rare moments she gives it to me.

Johnnie's head lolls from side to side. Both dried and fresh blood mar his battered and bruised face. His eyes are swollen to the point he can't see my fist flying in his direction, and gashes litter his cheeks and nose. His dirty clothes were better off before I got my hands on him, and I would say he's getting close to being unrecognizable.

And I haven't even gotten to the good stuff yet.

Since we arrived at my house two hours ago, and I tied him to a chair in the center of my basement, all he has known is pain. I refused to speak, wanting him to sit in constant fear and anxiety as he waits for my next move. I want him to feel as scared as Paetyn was the night he tried to mug her.

I squat in front of Johnnie and scan his deformed features. A grin splits across my face. "Tell me something, Johnnie."

His voice trembles as he says, "An-anything you w-want. Just p-please don't h-hurt me anymo-re." A cough rumbles deep in his throat, and blood splatters on my black jeans, joining the rest of his droplets.

"Why did you attack my little bird, hm? Were you looking for a quick buck to buy more drugs? Alcohol? Or did you want to hurt her because she was at the right place at the right time?"

His shoulders stiffen, his body unmoving as his breathing grows shallow. "I-I don't—"

"I'm going to stop you right there, Johnnie." I reach into my back pocket and produce my favorite switchblade. The blade slicing through the air as I flip it open is almost deafening. And now Johnnie is shaking like a leaf. "If you lie to me about your intentions, and trust me, I will know, I won't hesitate to take your fingers, one at a time, until you tell me the truth." I stand to my full height, staring down at the rat before me. "Now, answer the question. Why her?"

Johnnie pulls at the rope binding his wrist to the wooden chair, but it's no use. He's not fucking going anywhere.

"Pl-please don't hurt me. I can't take much—"

His scream pierces the air the moment my blade begins tearing through the tendons of his forefinger. But I don't get the pleasure of getting all the way through when his voice stops me in my tracks.

"I was paid to do it!"

With my blade halfway through the bone in his finger, I pause, my gaze flicking to meet his sweaty, blood-covered face. "What did you just say?"

"Some guy paid me to mug her, okay?" he explains, his words frantic as he wheezes. "Plea-se believe me."

"I do." But just because I believe him doesn't mean I'm not going to go through with cutting off the rest of his finger. So, I do. The severed appendage falls to the ground at my feet as his painful cries fill the damp basement, his body writhing in agony.

I wipe the bloody blade on my thigh before slipping it back into my pocket. "So, someone paid you. Who?"

Tears stream down Johnnie's face as he struggles to breathe, snot and saliva mixing with the blood coating his face. "I-I don't know his name, o-or remember his face."

"Do you remember anything about him?"

He shakes his head. "He was wearing a hood, concealing his face." Johnnie groans, his head lulling backward and forward as he fights consciousness. "He... he paid me a hundred bucks to mug her. He even gave me a date, time, and location... but provided no other information."

I hum as I consider his words. I was hired by an unknown buyer through Enzo to kidnap Paetyn and was given strict instructions not to harm her. That was my only requirement. I thought the job was weird at first but couldn't pass up the payday being offered. Normally, Enzo has me complete missions that will end in a lot of bloodshed, but this was the first one where I didn't have to kill anyone, and all I had to do was keep her at the house.

But although the job was completed without a hiccup, I haven't been able to fully let my little bird go.

Who is out there trying to hurt Paetyn?

If it was the same guy who hired me, why didn't he go back to Enzo? Johnnie is clearly not a professional like me, just a common street thug, so why the downgrade? With his lack of experience, he could have easily hurt Paetyn if she were to have fought back. He's lucky I got there when I did. Otherwise, I would've killed him on the spot for hurting a single hair on her head.

"Interesting," I murmur, cracking my split knuckles, relishing in the pain coursing up the length of my forearms. "If you had a name for me or facial features, I would have considered keeping you alive, but you have nothing else to offer me, so therefore, you're useless."

Johnnie tries to open his eyes as his body vibrates with fear, but they're too swollen. "Please do-don't. I'll do anything, j-just don't kill me."

I lower myself so we're at eye level. His cut bottom lip quivers as he waits for me to speak or make a move. I simply smile at him.

I wish he knew how much his fear gets me going.

"Maybe you should've thought about that before you touched what is mine. And now, I'm going to make you regret ever accepting that hundred bucks to hurt my little bird. It's going to be long and painful, so you better strap in for the ride."

The moment my fist connects with his broken cheekbone, blood explodes across the room, followed by whimpering and tears.

This better be a lesson to anyone he may have spoken to who thinks they can get their hands on Paetyn. My obsession with her is unlike anything I've ever felt. It's a rush I crave; I need it injected into me like a drug. She is constantly on my mind—her voice keeping me awake at night as I remember the feel of her body against mine and the way she says my name.

I refuse to let any harm come her way. If someone out there is trying to hurt her, they'd better fucking believe I'll be right there to put an end to it. Mark my words.

CHAPTER TWENTY-ONE

Paetyn

It's been a week since Liam accused me of cheating on him, and I hit him with the evidence I have collected of his supposed infidelity. Whenever we're in the same room, he refuses to look at me or utter a single word, choosing silence over discussing the situation at hand. Like a child.

In the four years I have been dating Liam, he has never once apologized for a fight or admitted he was in the wrong. I'm the one who has to apologize first and start talking to him again. Otherwise, if I don't, he will continue to play the silent game. And I can't stand it. Knowing he's in the same house, breathing the same air, and going about his day and not speaking to me makes me irate. He's sleeping in the spare bedroom for God's sake.

By now, I would've given in and apologized just so he would stop this game, but I refuse to be the bigger person this time, especially when he has been no saint either.

With a huff, I grab my car keys and head to the front door. Liam is at his parents' house, working on something with his father for his campaign. He has been over there a lot this past week. Not only has he been staying late at the office or been out on the campaign trail, he's been having dinner with his parents most nights, or he's out schmoozing with potential campaign donors, telling them I'm still too shook up from my ordeal to come along, leaving me home alone with my thoughts.

I'm sure his parents have questioned him about me and why I'm not with him. Given his close relationship with them, it wouldn't surprise me if he threw me under the bus but kept the details of his activities to himself.

I slide into the driver's seat and send a text message to Raya.

PAE: Hey, are you busy?

Her response comes quickly.

RAYA: I'm lying on the couch in my pajamas with a tub of ice cream beside me, so no, I'm not busy. What's up?

PAE: I need to get out of the house. Are you able to meet me at the mall? I could use some retail therapy and a distraction.

RAYA: Say less, Pae. I'll be there in thirty minutes.

The drive to the closest mall is about twenty-five minutes with traffic. By the time I get a parking spot and head in to wait at our usual meet-up point, Raya has just arrived with two coffees in hand.

She rushes up to me and hands me a cup. I accept it without hesitation. It's warm nestled against my palms, battling the chill racing through my body.

"Is everything okay?" Raya asks, her head tilted to the side. She's wearing jeans and a thick puffer coat, not wanting to take any chances with the New York weather.

I sip the coffee only to take a moment to form a response. Should I tell her what happened with Liam? And more importantly, Ace? She warned me away from Ace, saying I could find myself in danger given what he did to me, but I've done the exact opposite. If anything, I can't seem to stay away from him no matter how hard I try to ignore his presence or woodsy cologne. My attempts are futile.

"I'm okay." I force a smile on my face. "I just need a distraction."

"I'm more than happy to help you with that." Raya links her arm through mine and tugs me toward a shop. "Let's shop and talk."

We do just that.

While we walk aimlessly through clothing stores, picking up an item only to put it back when we realize we don't actually like it, we catch each other up on what we've been doing. Raya tells me about her job and a recent promotion she got. She gushes about Seren and how she thinks he's close to proposing. They've been dating for nearly five years, so it's bound to happen at any time, but Raya is convinced it'll be soon.

I couldn't be happier for my best friend. Not only does she have a good job and a caring partner, but she has her shit together, which is more than I can say for myself.

Raya drags me into another store to look at a pair of shoes she has been eyeing. She asks a worker to get the shoes in her size, and she settles onto a stool, her eyes gazing up at me expectantly.

"Okay, Pae, I've updated you on my life, so it's your turn. How is your mom? Liam? Your stalker?"

My body stiffens at the mention of Liam and Ace practically in the same sentence. Raya picks up on the reaction because her eyes widen, but she can't comment on it when the worker walks over with her shoes.

I use this time to decide what I should tell her about Liam and Ace. Should I tell her the truth or keep a lot of the details to myself? The only problem with lying to her is that she can see straight through any lie I tell. Nothing gets past her.

So, I have no choice but to tell her the truth.

When the worker walks away, Raya raises a brow at me. "Spill, Pae."

I blow out a long breath. "Okay, well, Mom is doing good. I had a call with her doctor this morning, and he said she's responding to the treatment well. Liam and I haven't spoken in a week after he accused me of cheating on him, and it happened to be the same night I slept with my stalker… again."

The words tumble from my mouth, and I'm helpless to stop them.

Raya's jaw pops open as she stares at me, wide-eyed. Her body is still as she gapes at me, at a loss for words.

"I know what you're going to say. I know. What I did is fucked up, and Liam has every right to be pissed with me, but he has been cheating on me for months. I'm not saying it to justify my actions, but I don't want to be perceived as the only bad guy in this situation."

She swallows hard, regaining her composure after the bomb I just dropped. Raya stands and grabs my hands, holding them tightly in hers. "Pae… woah, that was a lot. But I don't think you're a bad person for what you did."

My heart thumps harshly in my chest. "You don't?"

Raya shakes her head, strands of strawberry blonde hair flying around her face. "No, I don't. I know I told you to stay away from your stalker because he sounds dangerous, but there must be a reason you gravitate toward him."

"I don't know why I can't stay away from him," I admit quietly. "I mean, yes, he's insanely attractive, but I feel safe when I'm with him like nothing or no one can hurt me. And when I'm with him… he makes me feel alive."

"Has Liam ever made you feel either of those things?"

I shake my head without hesitation. "I know what I'm doing is wrong and fucked up, but it's as if my body is demanding one thing and my heart is slowly giving in to that desire. I shouldn't even be thinking of the notion of choosing between my fiancé and my stalker because the right answer is staring me in the face, but it's not what I want."

"What do you want, Pae?" Raya asks, her voice gentle.

"I want a partner who will protect me and put me first." The admission shocks me, making my heart beat faster. I've never admitted out loud how I wish Liam was more of the manly type who would do anything to ensure my safety instead of having someone else look out for me. But after meeting Ace, and knowing the lengths he will go to in order to keep me safe, it's something I desire. I know I can look after myself, but having a partner who is willing to go the extra mile for you and put you ahead of everything and everyone makes my stomach flip excitedly.

"If I leave Liam…" I swallow hard, the words getting caught in my throat, "I won't be able to care for my mother. It's not something I can afford with my salary, and the last thing I want is to jeopardize my mom's health. But Ace… at the end of the day, he's a criminal, and that's not something I should get myself mixed up in either, no matter what he makes me feel."

Raya nods, understanding the predicament I'm in. "It doesn't help that you're a somewhat well-known face in New York with Liam running for office, so there is the added element of causing a media storm. And if you get involved with this Ace guy, you could be walking into a very dangerous world that could land you in some trouble."

She hit the nail on the head with that one.

"No matter who I choose, there isn't going to be a great outcome for me."

Raya smiles, the gesture laced with empathy. "I suppose it will come down to who you want more, and you can make your decision from there. But it's not something you have to do right now, okay? Let's keep shopping and forget about men."

I swallow hard and nod. Although, now that I've opened the can of worms that is the shit show of my life, I'm unsure if I can stuff them back inside and forget about them. But I'm sure as hell going to try.

Raya purchases the shoes, giddy as a kid on Christmas morning. When we step out of the store, arms linked, I'm immediately blinded by flashing lights. I stumble back, held up by Raya, and try to adjust my eyes to whatever light is shining in my eyes.

"Paetyn, how are you doing after the kidnapping?"

"Have they found the man who did this to you?"

"How has your fiancé Senator Aster been supporting you through this terrible time?"

"How did Senator Aster find you? Is he your hero?"

"Do you have any comments on your fiancé's campaign?"

My blood runs cold as I realize what is happening. Their voices rain down on me like a thunderous storm, threatening to consume me. I haven't had to deal with the media since the kidnapping because Liam was right there to distract them by answering their questions on my behalf. I'm not suitable to be in front of a camera because I tend to freeze up like I am right now, unable to speak.

But now I'm on my own without the help of Liam to get me through this.

Oh, no.

"She's not taking any questions right now," Raya answers for me. I'm grateful she is here, otherwise, I'd be fucked. "Now, take a step back so we can leave."

They don't take a step back. If anything, they throw more questions at me, blurring into one voice as it assaults my ears. After the conversation I just had with Raya, listening to the media ask me questions about Liam and Ace quickly becomes too much.

I have to get the hell out of here. Now.

I turn to Raya, my voice barely above a whisper. "I need to get out of here."

"Let me come with—"

"I need to be alone."

Raya regards me for a moment, her gray eyes filled with concern, but ultimately, she releases her arm from mine. "Be safe, okay? Call me if you need anything."

I manage a quick nod before I turn to the left and run toward the exit as fast as my legs will carry me. The media follows me but are quickly stopped by security, allowing me to escape. My heart thumps harshly in my chest as I push through the throng of people shopping, not caring when I bump their shoulders or nearly trip over my feet.

When I reach my car, I'm out of breath, but I don't stop. I climb in and take off. I merge easily with the traffic on the main road, my hands gripping the steering wheel so tightly that my knuckles begin to ache.

My first instinct is to go home and shut myself away in my bedroom, but being in the same space as Liam is the last thing I want. It's a cruel reminder that the man I've spent four years of my life with is refusing to speak to me.

Instead, I decide to go to the one place I know I shouldn't.

CHAPTER TWENTY-TWO

Ace

"How is everything with you, Ace?"

I blink at Enzo from across his desk, the leather seat cool against the back of my jean-clad thighs. He leans back in the large chair, his hands running down the front of his dark blue blazer sculpted to his frame. Not a single strand of dirty-blond hair is out of place, and his hard blue eyes focused on me.

"Everything is fine," I answer, my back pin-straight. "Is there any news on those Bonanno fuckers?"

"They've been silent," Enzo says and leans forward. "After they messed with our supply drop, it seems they've gone into hiding, likely waiting for us to retaliate."

"Are we going to retaliate?"

Enzo hums. "Not yet. Patience is a virtue. If they think we could strike at any moment, I want them to fester in that anxiety, waiting for the unknown."

I nod. Enzo isn't someone who rushes into a situation like this, guns blazing, ready to kill. He takes his time planning an attack down to the finest details. Partly because he likes to keep his enemy on edge, hoping they might slip up somewhere so he can use that to his advantage, but also partly due to him wanting control over the situation. If he wants a fight, he will ensure he is the one controlling every move made. It's something I respect about him.

"As always, I will be waiting for your orders."

Enzo grins, that same evil twinkle in his eyes I see every day. "And that's why I like you, Ace. Out of everyone in Gambino, I trust you the most. Not just because you're my enforcer, but I know I can count on you to get shit done and carry the gang when the going gets tough."

"I appreciate that," I say with a nod. "Always happy to serve you."

He leans back in the chair, a satisfied smile turning up his mouth. "Now that's what I like to hear. You can go now."

I stand but hesitate, locking eyes with Enzo. "I have a question before I go."

Enzo opens his arms, gesturing toward me. "Hit me with it."

"Who was the buyer who hired me to kidnap Paetyn Jones?"

He stares at me for a beat, his tongue poking the inside of his cheek as he regards me. I'm not one to care about buyers and what they ask of me, but when it concerns my little bird, I'm not going to stop until I know who the fucker is.

"Why do you want to know that?" he finally asks, his tone shifting to one of curiosity.

"I just want to know why someone would pay to kidnap her only to release her unharmed."

Enzo exhales a long breath and folds his hands over his chest. "Well, as much as I would like to share those details with you, Ace, it's not something you need to know. As my enforcer, I need you to focus on the jobs I give you, not some girl, okay?"

My jaw clenches, and it takes everything in me not to tell Enzo that Paetyn isn't just 'some girl.' She's my girl. But if I do, he will know I'm lying about not being in contact with her after the job was completed. The last thing I need is a pissed-off Enzo.

"Okay," I say through my teeth.

Before I can turn and leave, Frank, Enzo's head of security, bursts into the room. His aged features are set into a hard frown, his back straighter than wood. "Boss, we need you in the control room."

Enzo stands and lays his hands on the desk. "What's going on?"

"We think some members of Bonanno have been stalking the premises."

"Those fuckers," Enzo curses under his breath. He walks out from behind his desk and locks eyes with me. "Keep your head on straight, Ace."

The warning clings to me as I watch him leave the room, not waiting to see if I follow. I've been with Enzo for many years, and never once has he given me a warning like that. It should concern me that he knows something is going on, but I don't care enough to put his mind at ease. At the end of the day, when I'm not protecting Enzo, I'm watching out for my little bird. And that means finding out who the fuck paid to have her kidnapped.

I glance at the open door to the office, checking for signs of anyone passing by, before I reach into my pocket, producing a USB drive. The desktop on Enzo's desk is open, so I get to work downloading all the documents from previous buyers in the last three months. My eyes flick between the screen and the open door, hoping Enzo doesn't return before I have what I need.

Betraying Enzo like this is something I wouldn't have done a few months ago. I'm loyal to a fault and will do anything for him, but I'm no longer the same man I once was. Not after Paetyn stumbled into my life. Now, I will do anything to protect her, even if it means risking the family I have built within the Gambino gang.

Once all the files are securely on the USB, I retrieve it from the computer and ensure the mouse is exactly where Enzo left it. I slip the USB into my pocket and straighten my jacket before leaving the room, closing the door behind me.

I hear Enzo and Frank in the control room as I pass by, their voices muffled by the closed door. With my chin tipped up, I walk through the mansion and out to my car. Once I get home, I will comb through every document and find the fucker responsible for Paetyn's kidnapping and make them wish they had never made the transaction.

* * *

A HEAD OF SILVER HAIR IS THE FIRST THING I NOTICE WHEN I PULL INTO the driveway. Paetyn sits on the front steps with her knees tucked up to her chest, her eyes following me as I get out of the car.

"What are you doing here, little bird?" I gaze down at her, unable to believe my eyes that she's here on her own accord.

Paetyn stands, the top of her head barely reaching my chin. She wraps her arms around her waist, meeting my eyes. "I didn't want to go home, and somehow, I ended up here. Is that okay?"

My fingers twitch at my side, desperate to touch her, hold her, but I don't. I don't want to push her away when she has willingly come to me. "You don't even need to ask. I couldn't be more pleased to see you."

"I just…." She exhales deeply and shifts on her feet. "I don't know what I'm doing."

"Do you want to come inside?" I offer as I step past her to unlock the front door. "I can get you a drink or something to eat."

Paetyn silently follows me into the house, waiting by the front door as I flip on the lights. When I turn to her, a fire simmers in the depths of her emerald eyes. "Actually, I was looking for more of a… distraction. I need something to take my mind off everything."

My cock twitches, and I grin, unable to hide my pleasure at hearing the subtle double meaning in her words. "You want a distraction? Well, it just so happens that I have something in mind, little bird."

CHAPTER TWENTY-THREE

Ace

I step forward, my eyes locked with hers. "Tell me what you want."

Paetyn blinks at me, those soft green eyes piercing through my soul. "You," she murmurs, her voice as sweet as her scent.

Fuck me.

That one word would be my undoing.

Everything about this woman is intoxicating and messes with my fucking head. All I want is to keep her locked up in this house so she will never have to leave me again or go home to the cheating fucker who doesn't deserve her.

Hell, I don't deserve her, but I'm selfish enough to keep her.

"Me?" I say, rolling the word around my mouth as I brush my chest against hers. She shudders, but holds my gaze. My hand grazes hers, the heat from her skin lighting a fire in my veins. "And what do you want me to do, little bird? Say the word and I'll make it happen."

She swallows hard, strands of silver hair falling delicately around her soft features. Paetyn is the most beautiful woman I have ever had the pleasure of laying eyes on. Anytime another man looks in her direction, it takes every ounce of self-control I have to not rip their eyes from their skull. But that would land in a load of trouble I didn't want to deal with. But it didn't stop me from imagining the scenario in my head as I watched from a distance, ensuring her safety.

If she so much as asked me to jump, I wouldn't fucking hesitate to say how high.

"Can we…" Paetyn clears her throat and wrings her hands in the small space between our bodies. "Go up to your room?"

"And do what?"

Her cheeks turn a light shade of pink and she drops her eyes to the ground. "Don't make me say it, Ace."

I bite back a smile at how adorable she is when she's embarrassed. I know exactly what she wants. When I opened the chest in my room the last time she was here, revealing a side to me not many women have had the privilege to see, I saw the way her eyes lit up with excitement and curiosity. It was as if I had unlocked a whole new world for her, one she didn't know she craved.

It took everything in me not to go all in that night and push her limits. But I knew I would be playing with fire if I had. Considering she had likely never been tied up before, especially not with that vanilla-ass motherfucker she's dating, I didn't want to push the boundaries of what she was comfortable with.

The moment I bound her hands behind her back and heard the hitch in her breath as her body trembled with excitement and anticipation, I knew I had unlocked a hidden desire she didn't know she possessed. And ever since that night, I haven't been able to stop thinking about how fucking stunning she looked in that position with her ass in the air, pussy dripping for *me*. Every sound she made for *me* has been playing on a loop in my mind like a fucking broken record, and I've been dying to add to the collection.

I tuck a strand of silver hair behind her ear and cup her cheek, holding her gaze steady. "Okay, I won't. But I will make sure you're screaming my name with that pretty little mouth of yours."

Her eyes widen as excitement and desire cloud those pretty eyes of hers.

Without saying a word, I wrap my hands around the back of her thighs and hoist her up. At the same time her toned legs wrap around my waist, I attach my lips to hers, needing to fucking feel every inch of her. I didn't get the chance to kiss her last time because I was too caught up in the moment, so I have a lot of catching up to do.

Our mouths clash in an inferno of heat and lust. My hands tighten around her thighs as I blindly walk to the staircase, taking each step from memory. Paetyn's hands are in my hair, tugging on the roots as her mouth moves effortlessly with mine. A soft groan sounds from the back of her throat when I swipe my tongue over her bottom lip.

If I wasn't a patient man, I would fucking take her right here on the staircase like a wild animal.

But she wants more, and I'm more than willing to give that to her.

I kick the door open to my bedroom and blindly feel for the light switch with one hand while the other moves to grip her perky ass, kneading the skin. That earns me a deep moan as light illuminates the room.

I reluctantly break the kiss to place her on the ground in front of the bed. We're both panting as we stare at each other, our chests heaving. Without breaking eye contact, I shove the coat off her shoulders. The material has barely hit the floor before I reach for the hem of her T-shirt and discard the item beside me.

My eyes rake over her impressive chest concealed by a red lace bra.

I finger the strap, tilting my head to the side. "Did you wear this just for me, little bird?"

Paetyn opens her mouth to respond, but the words die in her throat when I press my lips against hers, capturing the sounds like a greedy bastard. I make quick work of her jeans, shoving the material down her thighs until she was in nothing but her matching underwear.

God, this woman is fucking stunning. A work of art, really.

"Ace," she moans against my lips when I pull away, her breathing coming out in heavy pants. "Please."

"Please what?" I encourage as I take a step back, admiring the beauty before me. Every curve of her body and every freckle littering her creamy skin has already been committed to memory the moment I first laid eyes on her, but seeing her in this state brings with it a whole new wave of possessiveness that I can't ignore.

"Touch me," she whispers, her eyes searching my face. "Do whatever you want."

My eyes nearly bulge out of my head. "You—what?"

A sly grin turns up the corner of her mouth as she runs a hand down my chest, toying with the hem of my black T-shirt. "I'm all yours, Ace."

Fuck me.

This woman is going to be the death of me.

"That's a dangerous game you're playing," I strangle out, unable to get my fucking heart under control as she snatches it from my chest. "I hope you know that."

She nods as her hand slips beneath the fabric, gliding over the muscles in my abdomen. "I know."

"And you will be at my mercy."

"I know."

Fuck *me.*

I reach back to fist the fabric of my shirt before roughly tugging it over my head, letting it fall on the ground with the rest of Paetyn's clothes. "Don't say I didn't warn you, little bird."

Paetyn releases a low gasp when I hook a finger around the thin material of her panties and rip it from her body, the torn fabric joining the pile at our feet. Her heated eyes are on me when I reach behind her and expertly unhook her bra, the material falling away effortlessly.

A low hum sounds from my throat as I grab one of her perky tits in my hand, the skin smooth and soft against mine. Paetyn tips her head back as I roll the nipple between my fingers, pinching the rosy bud until she moans.

"Get on the bed," I order, my voice low. "Lie on your back and put your arms above your head."

A shudder rolls through her body before she exhales a shaky breath and turns on her heels. I watch with heated eyes and a painfully hard cock as she saunters around the bed and crawls onto the mattress, ass in the air and pussy dripping. She settles on her back and does as she's told, raising her arms above her head so they rest against the mound of pillows. Thick silver strands splay around her head like a halo.

This woman truly is a fucking angel.

I roll my shoulders back and walk over to the chest to the right of the bed frame. Paetyn's eyes follow my movement, watching with curiosity and anticipation. Since she has given me the green light to do whatever I like with her, I have something in mind that I know will drive her crazy.

With the vibrator and handcuffs in hand, I turn around, a lazy grin taking over. Paetyn's eyes widen upon seeing the two items in my hand and she wriggles on the spot, clenching her thighs together as her heated emerald eyes stay locked on me.

With two easy steps, I'm kneeling on the mattress beside Paetyn's head. I grip her right wrist and pull it toward the anchor attached to the wooden headboard. The handcuffs are metal but black fur lines the inside for comfort. Sliding the handcuff through the anchor, I secure one side around her wrist before reaching for the other and securing that one.

Leaning back to admire my handiwork, I strangle out a low growl at the sight of Paetyn's arms flush against her cheeks, pushing her perfect tits together. The thought of another man seeing her like this fills me with murderous thoughts, made worse by knowing she has a fiancé.

Not for much longer if I have anything to do with it.

"Comfortable?" I ask, dragging my tongue over my bottom lip.

Paetyn pulls against the restraint but is unable to move. Her eyes flick to me and I lose my breath at the sight of her flushed cheeks and heaving chest.

I'm fucking doomed.

"As I can be," she admits, her voice barely above a whisper.

"Good." I get off the bed and walk back to the chest, retrieving one last item. "I almost forgot this."

When I return to the bed, Paetyn's eyes widen at the black silk eye mask lying in my hand.

"You're going to blindfold me?" Her body is trembling, but I know it's from excitement and not fear. I can hear it in her voice.

"Is that a problem?" I ask as I kneel beside her, my head tilted to the side.

Her throat works to swallow whatever is in her mouth before shaking her head. "Not at all."

"Good, but you don't have much of a choice, remember?"

With that, I slip the mask over her eyes, focusing on the way her breathing grows heavy. My cock is aching to be freed from the confinement of my jeans, but I need to be patient. If my little bird wants a distraction, then I'm going to bring her a world of pain and pleasure that has her forgetting her name.

I grab the vibrator off the mattress and move to settle between Paetyn's thighs. They're clenched, but not for much longer. I place both hands on either side of her thighs and pry them apart, earning a sharp gasp from Paetyn. Losing the ability to see will heighten each move I make, leaving her wondering what I'm going to do next.

"If you close your legs, I'm going to punish you."

Paetyn exhales a shaky breath and nods.

I trace a finger up her inner thigh and through her slick folds, arousal coating my skin. "Good girl." I pull away and slip my finger between my lips, desperate for a teasing taste of her.

She's the best damn thing I've ever tasted.

The vibrator switches on, the sound almost deafening in the room. Paetyn swallows hard, fighting the urge to wriggle where she lays. I grin as I lower the device to her dripping pussy. The moment the spinning head touches her, a loud cry bursts from her lips as she pushes her head back against the pillows. It's on the lowest setting and yet it's driving her crazy.

"You like that?" I groan out, unable to take my eyes off the way her body trembles and her fingers curl into her palms. "Do you want more?"

Paetyn nods, her bottom lip tucked harshly between her teeth as she presses herself further into the mattress.

Just when her toes begin to curl, an orgasm fast approaching, I pull the vibrator away. Paetyn cries out in frustration over the loss of contact, which only makes me grin from ear to ear.

Oh, this is going to be fucking fun.

"What was that?" I offer. "I asked if you wanted more but got no answer."

"Please, Ace," Paetyn moans, chest heaving with each breath. "Give me more."

"Your wish is my command."

I return the vibrator to her pussy and watch as her body writhes under the vibration, desperately chasing a release I'm not going to give. *Yet.* Paetyn moans, the sound like fucking music to my ears as she fights to keep her legs apart.

I'm itching to reach out and touch her, taste her, fucking claim her. But I hold back only because I know once I do get my hands on her, I won't be able to stop myself from taking every last inch of her for myself. I'm a fucking depraved man when it comes to this woman, so I need to reign in the beast for a little longer while I play with her.

Much like before, just when she is about to come, I pull the vibrator away.

"What the fuck, Ace," she growls, panting. The frustration of being brought to the edge only to be snatched away is evident in her voice and the way she's likely shooting daggers at me through the eye mask.

I smirk, unable to stop myself. "What? Is there something you want?"

"Yes," she groans, voice ragged. "I want you to fuck me."

Good lord. Her words are like a bolt of electricity straight to my cock.

"Is that right?" I hum, turning the vibrator over in my hand.

"Please," she whines, her tongue darting out to swipes across her bottom lip. "I need you."

My heart slams against my rib cage and all plans to drive her crazy go out the fucking window. Those three words are like a nuclear bomb going off in my chest. Who knew hearing her say something as simple as that would be enough to break my resolve and shove logic out the window?

I'm fucking done for.

With a grunt, I drop the vibrator on the mattress beside me and hastily unbutton my jeans. A growl bursts from my throat the moment I pull out my painfully hard cock, my eyes locked on her naked frame lying sprawled out over my bed.

"Come here." I grab both of her ankles and tug her forward, stretching her arms further. She cries out at the sudden change in pressure on her shoulders. "You asked for this, little bird. Begged me even."

"Ace," she moans, squeezing her thighs against my waist as I pump my cock. "*Please.*"

"Fuck," I hiss, all patience out the fucking window.

I shove a hand through my hair before gripping her ankles and tugging them up so they rested on my shoulders, lining her pussy up with my cock. The crown nudged her entrance, slicking me with her arousal. Paetyn groaned as I slide deeper, her walls tightening around me like a fucking warm blanket.

When I bottom out, my head drops forward and a groan bursts from my lips. Once I've caught my breath, I reach for the vibrator again and switch it on. Paetyn struggles against the handcuffs when the sound reaches her.

"What are you doing?" Her voice is barely above a whisper. "Ace?"

I don't respond with words and instead growl as I lower the device to her pussy, reveling in the way she tips her head back and cries out my name.

I feel like a deranged beast as I draw my hips back to drive into her at a punishing pace while the vibrator works her clit. An ungodly sound falls from her mouth as I fuck her, the double boost of pleasure quickly driving her to the brink of no return.

Strands of inky waves fall over my eyes as I focus on where our bodies connect and the black vibrator dancing over her swollen nub. A filthy groan sounds in the air as I grip her hip with my free hand, angling her body to allow me to drive into her deeper, hitting the spot I know drives her crazy.

Our harsh breathing mixes in a symphony of lust that only adds to the fire burning deep in my core. Paetyn cries out my name and fists her hands tightly as she receives each punishing thrust. Her perky tits bounce wildly, drawing my attention to them before I sweep my gaze upward to the plump lights formed in a tight O.

This woman is fucking perfection. And she's all mine.

"Come on my cock, Pae," I ground out, struggling to hold on.

Paetyn is a breathless mess as she writhes beneath me, body trembling as she dashes to the edge. She opens her mouth to speak, but only a puff of air escapes.

Moments later, her walls tighten around my cock, stealing every ounce of air from my lungs as she comes on my cock. Her legs shake on my shoulders as she cries out my name.

I growl as I slam into her, increasing the intensity of her orgasm as I chase my own. Every muscle in my body is wound tight as I thrust into her one last time before exploding. I drop my head as I empty inside of her, sweat slicking my skin and my breathing ragged.

My vision blurs at the edges as I try to gather myself. The room is silent besides our harsh breathing, neither of us making a move to speak or move a muscle.

I flick my eyes up to Paetyn where she lay perfectly still, her breathing slowly evening out, her lips slightly parted. Her smooth skin is covered in a light sheen of sweat, and I would love nothing more than to lick every inch of her perfect body.

"Fucking hell," I murmur as I pull out of her, already missing the connection we just shared. "What the hell are you doing to me?"

When Paetyn doesn't respond, my brows crease. Sliding her legs off my shoulders, I move to her side and pull back the sleeping mask. To my surprise, her eyes are closed. She makes no move to open them.

I lean back and study her for a moment, realization slowly creeping in.

Did she pass out because of the intensity with which I fucked her?

I chuckle lowly and shake my head. Well, this is a first for me. But a valid one considering Paetyn is new to this world and just how intense it can be. She doesn't know just how far I'm capable of pushing a person beyond their limits. But I can't blame her for succumbing to exhaustion after being on such a high. If she is going to be with me, it's something I'm going to have to get her used to.

I release her from the constraints of the handcuffs and settle her on the pillows like the delicate flower she is. The back of my knuckle grazes over her flushed cheeks as I admire every detail of her face, unable to look away. I lean forward to press my lips to her forehead, savoring the scent of coconut shampoo and the warmth of her skin.

She truly has fucked up my life in a way I never thought possible. Before her, I was controlled and calm. But ever since she blew through me like a fucking hurricane, I'm anything but calm. All I want to do is protect her and never let her out of my sight. My obsession with wanting to be with her every second of every day is borderline delusional and possibly criminal, but I don't give a fuck. I would do anything for this woman if she asked, without hesitation.

Somehow, she reached into my chest, tore my black heart from where it sat, and shoved it into her pocket. I don't think she knows she has done it, but she will soon. In fact, I want her to keep it forever because I have no plans to ever let her go.

And I will pry her from that motherfucker's cold, dead hands if I have to.

CHAPTER TWENTY-FOUR

Paetyn

I'm greeted by harsh rays of moonlight shining through the open window above the bed when my eyes flutter open, heavy with sleep. Every muscle in my body is tense, my back aches and my limbs feel like a weight is keeping them pressed firmly against the mattress.

I force myself into a seated position, dragging the thin black sheet up to my chest. My eyes sting as I rub the sleep from them, hoping it'll make me feel more awake when in reality, I want to lie down and go back to sleep. I want to feel Ace's arms wrapped around me, holding me close to his firm chest as he strokes my hair.

Ace...

My eyes widen as panic crashes through me, nearly knocking the wind out of my lungs.

Ace!

I nearly get whiplash from the ferocity of my head snapping to the left where my phone sits on the bedside table. With my heart in my throat, I snatch the device off the table. The screen beams to life, almost blinding me in the dark room.

10:18 PM.

My heart sinks to my toes at the notifications on the home screen —ten missed calls and fifteen text messages from Liam.

Oh, shit....

I fling the sheet off my naked body, adrenaline guiding my legs around the room, searching for the clothing Ace threw everywhere. As I shove my legs into my jeans, I can only imagine what is going through Liam's mind right now. I left earlier while he wasn't home and didn't tell him when I would get back. He already thinks I'm cheating on him, so my not being home at this hour only fuels whatever scenarios are racing through his mind.

Even if I could find a way out of this situation, I know it's useless to try. Denying the attraction I feel for Ace would be futile, as it seems I always find myself gravitating toward him when I know I shouldn't. He's a dangerous man, and I shouldn't want him, but I do. I can't continue to fight whatever is forming between us.

Now, I have no choice but to go home and face the music.

I finish getting dressed and shove my phone into my jeans pocket and look at the messy bed, my brows furrowed. After I fell asleep, I didn't notice Ace leave my side. I whirl around, my gaze sliding across the empty bedroom.

Where is he?

Using the little light streaming in from the window, I walk to the closed door and pull it open. The upstairs hallway is dark, save for a light shining from beneath two doors down to my right. My footsteps are light as I make my way to the closed door. I consider walking in without knocking, but I'm not sure what Ace is doing in there, so it would be rude of me not to at least signal my presence.

I rap my knuckle on the wooden door three times before twisting the handle. When I step into the room, surrounded by bookshelves lining the walls on either side of me, I find Ace sitting behind a large mahogany desk, his gaze lifting from the laptop open in front of him to me.

"Little bird." Ace leans back on the leather desk chair, his chest bare and the strands of inky hair a mess atop his head. "You should be sleeping."

"So should you," I counter, walking further into the room.

He points at me, his head tilted to the side. "Why are you fully clothed and not naked? I didn't say I was done with you yet."

My cheeks warm as I stand beside him. "What are you doing?" I ask instead, pointing at the screen. From where I'm standing, I can't make out what he's reading, but it looks like paperwork of some sort.

Ace pokes the side of his cheek with his tongue, his intense gaze sliding across my face. The harshness of his features and the tension coursing through his body reignite the fire in my core. I thought I had gotten my fix of him tonight, but it seems just one look from him has me crumbling at his feet.

"Nothing that concerns you, little bird."

Apart from the fact that Ace kidnapped me and has been stalking me ever since I was rescued, I don't know much about him. I don't know what he does for work, what he enjoys doing in his spare time, or the little details that make up his personality. Getting to know a person all over again after I started dating Liam is not something I thought I'd ever have to do.

"Tell me about yourself," I say, resting my hands on his bare shoulders. The muscles tense beneath my touch but loosen after a second. Ace leans his head back, his eyes meeting mine. "I don't know anything about you. What do you do for work?"

"If I tell you, will you leave me?"

"That depends on what you do. If you're an accountant, I may have to leave for fear of boredom."

Ace bites back a smile. "I'm definitely not an accountant."

I squeeze his shoulders, and he sighs at the gesture. "Then you have nothing to worry about. I'm not leaving, Ace. You can tell me."

He holds my gaze for a moment, his jaw ticking as he considers my words. After everything that has happened between us, learning what he does for work is the last thing I'm worried about.

"I'm an enforcer for the Gambino gang. I hurt people for a living."

My first instinct should be to run and never look back because what normal person isn't afraid of someone who admits they're in a mafia gang and hurts people without so much as batting an eye? Not me. If Ace had told me this the first day I woke up in that cabin, I would have shaken in my boots and stayed as far away from him as possible.

But as I've spent more time with him, and he's proven to me that he would never hurt me, I'm not afraid of him. If anything, I feel safe with him. He kept me fed and hydrated in the cabin, he watched from afar when I left work at night and made sure I got home safe, and he even saved me from the mugger in the alleyway. Ace's actions and ability to protect someone may not be conventional in the sense of what is acceptable in society, but it's how he shows someone he cares. I can't fault him for that.

"When did you start working with them?"

Ace's eyes widen slightly at my question and lack of physical reaction, but he doesn't dwell on it. He reaches his right hand back to rest over mine, his thick silver ring cool against my skin. "When I was twenty-one. I would often compete in underground fight clubs for the adrenaline rush of hurting someone. I was addicted. It was enough to pay the bills, so I kept going back, chasing that rush. That's where Enzo found me and offered me a job as his enforcer. I couldn't pass up the opportunity to live comfortably while continuing to feel the rush I needed."

"And do you..."

"Kill people?" He raises a brow at me, finishing my sentences. "Yes, I do. All the time. Bad people, little bird."

I swallow hard. I have never met a person who has killed someone, let alone someone who does it for a job. It's an odd feeling to look someone like that in the face, knowing what they're capable of. While I don't condone killing people, I can't change this side of Ace. It's part of who he is, and I don't want him to change that about himself for me. He says he kills bad people, and I believe him, so I'm willing to push the details to the back of my mind where it's easier to pretend he doesn't have the blood of others on his hands.

"Why me?" I ask, my throat thick with nerves. It's a question I have been searching for the perfect time to ask. "Why did you kidnap me?"

Ace turns his attention to the screen and drops his hand from mine. He clicks through a few more documents. "That's what I'm trying to find out, little bird. Someone is out to hurt you, and I will stop at nothing to find out who."

"What do you mean?" My heart hammers in my chest. "Did… did someone pay you to kidnap me?"

A wave of emotions I can't keep track of crashes over me, making my head spin. How is this possible? Why would someone do this to me?

I thought I had been in the wrong place at the wrong time and became Ace's target the night he kidnapped me. I figured he didn't hurt me because he liked me. Maybe he'd planned to ransom me or something. I didn't know for sure. But nothing I thought was true seems to be the case. It was staged–and all because someone had paid him–or his boss, anyway–to do it.

Why?

The question won't stop repeating in my mind, like a drum beating mercilessly against my skull as I try to sift through the details I learned. Nothing seems to make sense as if there is a single piece of the puzzle missing that could give me the full picture.

Before Ace can respond, he lingers on a document dated two weeks before the night I was kidnapped. My name is in the subject line, followed by the details of what needed to be carried out. My heart nearly leaps from my chest at the price listed.

One hundred thousand dollars.

"What the fuck," Ace mutters as he skims the document.

We both see it at the same time, and it feels like I have been punched in the stomach, time moving slowly around me. All the air leaves my lungs as I stare at the name scribbled messily at the bottom of the document, signing an agreement to have me kidnapped for a hundred grand.

A name I know all too well, and one I was willing to take as my own when I said yes.

Liam Aster, my soon-to-be husband.

CHAPTER TWENTY-FIVE

Paetyn

Ace's voice sounds like static in my ears as I blink at the screen, one, two, three times, trying to process what I'm seeing right now.

My fiancé hired a mafia enforcer to kidnap me... Why? Why would he do something like that? It's not adding up, but the evidence is staring me right in the face.

"That motherfucker," Ace seethes, his balled fists on his thighs turning white. "I knew he was fucking hiding something."

I'm snapped out of my daze when Ace stands, shoving the chair back so hard it crashes against the wall behind us. Before he can take a step, I wrap my hand around his wrist. His body is vibrating under my touch, and fury seeps into his ocean eyes, turning them darker than I have ever seen them.

If I were to let him go, I have no doubt he would go after Liam.

Maybe even kill him. But hurting Liam isn't going to change what he did. With him being a politician, he has a lot of eyes on him. He's a household name at this point, so if Ace were to do something, I can't guarantee he won't get caught. Liam's father is a very powerful man, so he would make sure Ace paid for his crimes. And given what I've learned about Ace and being part of the Gambino gang, I imagine an all-out war would erupt.

All because of me.

I shake my head. "Ace, don't. I know you're angry, and believe me, I'm getting there, but you can't go after him."

He searches my face, his jaw ticking. "He had me hired to kidnap you. I should have his head just for even thinking of bringing you harm. I'm going to make him wish he had never approached Enzo or gone through with whatever sick plan he had."

I wrap my other hand around the same wrist, tugging him forward until his chest is pressed firmly against mine. Ace responds to my touch immediately, the fury slipping from his eyes ever-so-slightly as the tension in his muscles dissipates.

He pulls his wrist from my grip to cup my face. His skin sizzles against mine, and I find myself leaning into his touch, seeking comfort. After what I learned about my fiancé, I need support now more than ever.

"I'm going to make him pay for this, little bird," Ace whispers against my lips.

"I know," I murmur, my pulse thumping in my throat. "But I need to speak with him first. I think it's time we put everything out on the table. I need to hear him admit that he did this."

He scans my face, searching for something, but I'm not sure what. The curve of his jaw ticks before he swoops down to capture my lips. I instinctually wrap my arms around his neck, leaning into him for support as he steals my breath away.

The kiss is intense as Ace dominates my lips, claiming me with each swipe of his tongue and every time he nibbles on my bottom lip. And I let him because there is no point in fighting it anymore. Ace is the man I never knew I needed in my life. Not only does he protect me, but he puts me first every single time, and that's more than I could say for Liam.

I'm breathless when I pull away. Ace lowers his forehead against mine as his thumb drags across my swollen bottom lip. "That fucker is going to know you're mine, little bird. Fucking *mine*." He pulls his hand away, but not before dragging it down the base of my throat. "Give me the word, and I'll fucking kill him. If he so much as touches you—"

"I'll be fine," I interject, my voice barely above a whisper. "If I need you—"

"You'll let me know right away," he finishes for me, leaving me no room for argument.

I nod. "Okay."

Ace presses a chaste kiss to my swollen lips before releasing me. I exhale a long breath, turn on my heels, and leave without looking back.

The air outside is cold against my cheeks as I race to my car parked on the street. As each mile ticks by, and the closer I get to the house I share with Liam, the quicker my pulse races. I think I'm still in shock over what I learned about Liam and haven't had a chance to process it properly.

Anger is the first emotion I register. Why would my fiancé do something like that to me?

Betrayal follows close behind. How could someone I have spent four years of my life with plan something like this? And why?

None of this will make sense until I confront him with what I know.

By the time I arrive home, it's close to 11:00 PM and I'm simmering with anger and confusion. My muscles are tense and my back tight as I fling the car door open and stomp up the driveway. When I enter the house, I hear shuffling in the kitchen, indicating Liam is home and awake.

Without kicking my shoes off, I march down the hallway. Liam is standing in front of the kitchen island, his eyes locked on me when I enter. His hair is styled neatly away from his face, and he's dressed in a white linen button-down and dark brown slacks. His features twist in confusion when he sees me.

"Pae, where the hell have you—"

"Did you hire the Gambino gang to kidnap me?" The words tumble from my mouth, filling the space separating us.

Liam blinks at me, his face paling ever-so-slightly before he replaces it with a blank expression. "What are you talking about?"

"You know exactly what I'm talking about." I fold my arms over my chest, holding his gaze from across the island. "Don't bullshit me, Liam."

He runs a hand through his hair, his mouth opening and closing as he tries to form a response. After a moment, he huffs and shifts on his feet. "I didn't do it to hurt you, Pae."

"Then why did you do it?" I cry, throwing my hands in the air. "Why did you have me kidnapped? It doesn't make sense."

"I had to!" he shouts, his cheeks turning red as he stares back at me, his gray eyes wild. "I needed something to gain the public's attention. It had to be something big so I could rescue you, and in turn, draw more attention to my campaign and get more voters. The plan was perfect."

My jaw drops open at his admission, my vision blurring at the edges. "Did… did you just say you organized for me to be kidnapped so you could rescue me and look like a hero in the media? Local politician saves his fiancée? Are you fucking kidding me, Liam?"

A wave of nausea crashes in my stomach as I stare at the man I thought I was going to spend the rest of my life with. The same man who claims he loves me, would do anything for me, and couldn't wait to start a family with me.

Now, I see him as a man who used me as a goddamn pawn in his game to climb the political ladder, endangering me in the process all because he wanted to be a hero. A fucking hero.

"Paetyn…"

"No, I don't want to hear a goddamn word from you," I interject, anger simmering in my veins. "I can't believe you would stoop so low as to use me like that. What if I had been hurt? What then? You can't make yourself a hero if you never were one to begin with, Liam. You have to earn it, not take it."

Liam frowns, his features twisting in annoyance. "But you weren't hurt because I saved you, Pae. That was the point."

"That's beside the point!" Red blurs the edge of my vision, and every muscle in my body pulsates as I flex and unflex my fists at my sides, trying to control the high emotions tearing through my chest. "I'm not a pawn you can use in your game, Liam. I never consented to be a part of this plan. Did you ever stop to think about how being kidnapped would affect me? I was terrified that I would never see you, my mom, or Raya, again, and you were sitting at home without a care in the world. That's fucking sick."

"I did care," he says defensively, but the lack of emotion in his voice tells me otherwise. "At the end of the day, you came home safe and sound, and that's all that matters."

I scoff and shake my head, unable to look at him a second longer. "Yeah, I may have come home, Liam, but I'm no longer the same person."

The decision I had been toying with the past few weeks becomes clearer now, like the clouds have parted and sunshine consumes me. I know for a fact I won't regret what I'm about to do.

"We're over, Liam." My voice is so low I almost don't hear the words, but I know Liam did because his eyes widen.

"Paetyn… you don't mean that."

I rip the engagement ring from my finger and toss it at his chest. It clatters to the floor at his feet, but he doesn't take his eyes off me.

"The engagement is off, and I never want to see you again. I mean it." I take a step back. "I'll return to collect my things when I'm ready."

Liam steps around the island, his hands clenched at his side. He opens his mouth to speak, but no words come out.

Of course, he has nothing to say.

Before I can walk away, Liam's voice sounds behind me. "You're making a huge mistake, Paetyn."

I scoff and shake my head. "Leaving you is the best decision I could've made."

Once I walk out of this house, my life is going to change. I'll no longer be engaged, have a house, or support for my mother. But what I will have is the knowledge that I made the right choice.

And now, I have Ace. A man I didn't know I needed in my life, but I'm so glad he is.

When the front door slams shut behind me, closing the door to that chapter of my life, it hits me that I'm going to have to deal with the fallout of what I just did. Leaving Liam isn't going to be easy. I know far too much about his personal dealings that could be a problem for him. But I'm willing to take the risk.

When I'm back in my car, I dial Ace's number. He answers on the first ring.

"Pae, are you okay?"

I smile and lean my head back, a weight lifting off my shoulder. "I'm okay."

"He didn't hurt you, did he?"

I shake my head. "No, but I did call off the engagement."

I can almost hear Ace grinning through the phone. "That's my girl."

My cheeks grow warm. "Can I spend the night with you?"

A pause.

"Little bird, you never have to ask to spend the night with me. If you want to spend the rest of your nights with me, I'd be a happy man."

"Okay," I murmur. "Just so you know, Liam isn't going to let this go. I know what he's like."

"You will never have to worry about him so long as I'm around. I will stop at nothing to ensure your safety, you have my word."

I smile to myself. If Liam were to say those words to me, I would take it with a grain of salt because he never put me first or went out of his way to protect me. But when Ace says it, I know it's a promise he is willing to keep.

Ace is the devil in disguise, a walking sin, and I will gladly follow him into the fire.

Thank you for reading! Book 2 is coming soon!

ALSO BY BELLA MOONDRAGON

The Alpha King's Breeder series:
Bought by the Alpha: The Alpha King's Breeder Book 1
Loved by the Alpha: The Alpha King's Breeder Book 2
Lost by the Alpha: The Alpha King's Breeder Book 3
Luna of the Alpha: The Alpha King's Breeder Book 4
Legacy of the Alpha: The Alpha Kings's Breeder Book 5
Daughter of the Alpha: The Alpha King's Breeder Book 6
Descendants of the Alpha: The Alpha King's Breeder Book 7
Shadow of the Alpha: The Alpha King's Breeder Book 8
Son of the Alpha: The Alpha King's Breeder Book 9
Spare of the Alpha: The Alpha King's Breeder Book 10
Claimed by the Alpha: The Alpha King's Breeder Book 11
Atonement for the Alpha King: The Alpha King's Breeder Book 12
Rejected by the Alpha: The Alpha King's Breeder Book 13 (coming soon!)
The Luna's Vampire Prince series:
The Culling
The Kingdom
The Conquered
Wolf Shifter Fairy Tale Retellings series
Beauty and the Alpha Beast
Pregnant With Four Alphas' Babies
Chosen As the Breeder
Mated to Four Alphas
Threats Against the Breeder
At War for the Breeder

The Stolen Breeder

Four Alphas, Four Babies

Becoming the Luna Queen

Descendants of the Breeder

Desired by the Devil series

Whispers of the Devil

Banter of the Devil

Murmurs of the Devil

The Mafia Kings series

Indebted to the Mafia King

<u>Loved by the Mafia King</u>

Claimed by the Mafia King

Secrets of the Mafia King

Burned by the Mafia King

Kidnapped by the Mafia King (coming soon!)

Dark Stalker Romance series

Tempted by Sin

Fated by Sin (coming soon!)

Secret Billionaires series

Finding the Secret Billionaire by Olivia Bhelle Kildare

Falling for My Secret Billionaire by Bella Moondragon

Driven by the Secret Billionaire by ID Johnson

Wolf Shifter Alpha Kings series

Ravens and Ruins

Sundrops and Shadows

Snowflakes and Sabotage

The Vampire King's Feeder series

Claiming the Alpha's Daughter

Loving the Alpha's Daughter

Finding the Alpha's Daughter

Stand Alone Novels

One Weekend With the Billionaire

Shared by the Sexy Billoinaire Twins

Alpha of the Western Moon

Writing as B. Moon

The Boy Who Died

Sign up for Bella's newsletter here.

Or get a free novella from The Alpha King's Breeder series when you sign up here: The Beta and the Maid

Follow Bella on Facebook here.

Follow Bella on Bookbub here.